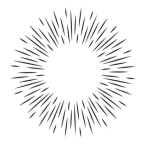

breathtobreath

craiglew

Afterword by Donna A. Gaffney, DNSc, PMHCNS-BC, FAAN

relish  media

Library of Congress Cataloging-in-Publication Data is available.
Library of Congress Catalog Card Number 2015942333

ISBN 978-1-939775-08-5

16 15 14 13 12 11   1 2 3 4 5 6 7 8 9 10

Little Pickle Press, Inc.
3701 Sacramento Street #494
San Francisco, CA 94118

Please visit us at www.littlepicklepress.com.

To William,

for your courage

to speak out,

to open up,

and to allow me in.

breathtobreath

Prologue

Live or die?
That's the question I ask
with every breath.
Continue to live,
or stop altogether?

Breathe

A breath only allows you to exist.
You must engage.
Venture forth.
Tangle yourself with others to have a life.
But life needs a purpose or what's the point?

Breathe

The point . . .

The point stares back at me.
Silver with gray lines where the machining sharpened it.
Nine inches of hardened steel.
A comfortable wood handle.
Only $4.99 at Bed Bath and Beyond.

Breathe

Beyond . . .

Beyond the optic nerve.
Cornea, iris, viscous body, retina.
If I get the ice pick beyond my eye,
I could reach the frontal lobe.
Where the memories live.
But I'll have to dig around
once the ice pick gets into my brain.
Swirl, dig, search, find
hideous memories hiding in their temple.

Breathe

Temple . . .

My temple.
The pterion bone is the thinnest spot
in our skulls, just behind our eyes
and in front of our ears.
I could go in sideways,
shove the ice pick straight in, then up.
Swirl, dig, search, erase.
But I might puncture the middle meningeal artery.
Does that matter? Not today.

Breathe

Today . . .

Today. Right now.
This very instant.
Who am I?

At any moment in time, we are the sum
of our experiences.
The average of our highs and lows
in the life we have played out.
The characters we have portrayed.
The truths we have embellished.
The lies we have told.
The facts we have omitted.
The life I once knew is all lies.

Breathe

Live or die?
Live or die?
Live . . . or . . .

Radar Dad

A train whistle blows. I jerk awake.

Clickety-clack, clickety-clack, clickety-clack

The *clickety-clack*
of the train on its track
is like a dose of NyQuil.

Side effects include
severe drowsiness
and mild nausea.

It's too early.
The sun, like me, is still not up.
My eyes are dry and tired.
I close them.

Clickety-clack, clickety-clack, clickety-clack

The mid-morning sunlight
pries my eyes open.
A family moves
toward me up the aisle.

Twin babies in a
double-wide stroller
bump the seats on
either side.
Their dark-haired mom
driving by Braille.

Behind them a smooth-
striding radar dad.

You know the type.
The dad
who constantly scans
for hot women
as he pretends
to be looking for
open seats.

What a dick.

He's trolling for chicks
using his kids as bait.

I continue watching him as
they parade past.

Sure enough, as women
smile at his kids,
he looks them up and down.
If one's worthy,
he pauses to tell
her the age of his kids,
all the while studying her
skin or butt or boobs.

Douche bag.

I hate that. Gives all us guys a bad rep.

I close my eyes again.

Clickety-clack,
            clickety-clack,
                        clickety-clack

Gum Chewer

Clickety-clack, clickety-clack, clickety-clack
Smack, smack, smack

I snap awake.
Gaze into huge blue eyes
belonging to a little girl about ten.

She's chewing cinnamon gum so loudly
her molars are going to fall out.

      "Do you still have your tonsils?" she asks.

"Um, yeah. Why?"

      "I knew it. I was looking at
      the back of your throat
      while you were sleeping."

"Ewwwww." Who is this kid?

      "Your mouth was wide open.
      It's like you were inviting me
      to look down inside."

"Actually, I don't believe I was."

      "You're drooling." She points at me.

"No I'm not."
But I wipe my chin with my sleeve.
"Ya know, it's not nice
to creep on people
while they're asleep."

"It's a public car," she exclaims.
"If you want to sleep,
why don't you go
to your sleeper room?"

"Cause I don't have one.
My grandma couldn't afford it."

She seems kind of embarrassed for me.
I hope she leaves me alone,
but I'm probably
the next youngest person with the ability
to form complete sentences on this train.

"I'm Emilia."
She air shakes my hand.

"Hi. I'm William."
I air shake back.

"Me and my mom got on at Santa Fe.
Where did you get on?"

"Kansas."

"Kansas? That's like all the way
on the other side of the country."

"Not really. Although, it feels like that right now."

"We're going to Disneyland.
Where are you going?"

"To live . . . with my dad."

Sketch

Emilia's conversation
whips up my homesickness.
I pull out my sketch pad
and the photo of Gramps
that G'ma gave me.

I can smell his Gray Flannel cologne
and Murphy's Beeswax pomade
when I look at his photo.

I push my pencil
across the toothy paper.
I outline Gramps' hair.
It's easy.

I sketch a good likeness of his ears,
but I can't seem to capture
the sparkle in his eyes
or the way he held his lips.

Like he was always about
to play a trick on you
or yell "boo!"

I cross out my attempt
and flip the page.

> "What are you drawing?" Emilia asks.
> "And yes, I'm still here."

"You read minds now?
Which princess are you?"

> "Princess?"

"You're going all this way to Disneyland.
You've got to have a favorite princess."

"Mulan. She kicked butt
and didn't need a prince
to save her."

"Good choice"
I get to work.
I imagine Emilia
as a Chinese princess
swinging a broadsword.

"Can I see?"

"No. You have to sit there
so I can sketch you."

I get lost in the picture.
My thoughts wander.
My emotions darken.

Poor G'ma.
She felt terrible
that I had to go.
There was no choice.
Not for me.
Not for her.

The sheriff made a deal with Gramps.
I either had to go to juvie
or leave.

It's not like the Edlebachers
didn't deserve it,
but everyone said
I went overboard.
Too far.

But no one heard Leela's screams
or saw her eyes pleading.
Yeah, my rage got the best of me.

I couldn't let those asshole brothers
hurt my friend, or worse.
Ryan's elbow doesn't work the same
and Jason could've died.
That would have been bad.

Right now I'm not sure I care.

     "Now can I see?"

"Sure. Here."
I rip the page out of my pad
and hand it to Emilia.

     "Wait.
     Are those heads?
     How cool!"

Emilia trundles off.
I close my sketch pad.

"Look, Mom." Emilia's voice pierces
through the *clickety-clack*.

"How horrible! Who drew this?"
I hear her mother squeal.

I guess Mulan wouldn't
chop off the heads
of all her friends.

I guess Emilia isn't sitting
with me any longer.

Text

My phone buzzes.

It's a text from J-Bob.

> HEY BUTTHEAD
> WHERE YAT?

JUST LEFT
NEW MEXICO

> ANY HOT CHICKS?

YES, IN FACT
YOU INTERRUPTED
MY CONVERSATION WITH EMILIA

> EMILIA? IS SHE LIKE 90?

CLOSER TO 9

> PERVERT

FUCK YOU

> YOU'D LIKE THAT

NO. YOU'RE TOO SKANKY

> I'VE WORKED HARD FOR THESE STDS

WHAT'S GOING ON TODAY?

TODD, KYLE, RUSSELL, AND ME
GOING TO ATOMIC

OF COURSE

I used to complain
how boring it was
that all my friends and I ever did
was go to the Atomic Bowling Alley
almost every day.

Now I'd give my left nut
to spend one more afternoon
with those dumbasses
in that dumbass place.

Train Stop

I haven't seen my dad
since I was four,
or at least that's what
Gramps told me.
Gramps said my dad couldn't
come see me
because of work.
Something to do with
national security and airports.

The only picture
I have of my father
is from his high school graduation
and that's blurry.

All I can really tell
is that he had long dark hair
and was rail thin.

I hope he's gained some muscle,
has a full head of hair,
and isn't suffering from arthritis,
high blood pressure, or
some other genetic bullshit.

I just want him to be happy to see me.

The train is stopping.
San Clemente.
My heart starts pounding.

I gather my duffel bag
and hop down onto the platform.
Here goes nothing.

Finding My Dad

Bodies,
movement,
cacophony,
chaos,
the end of summer heat, and
my growling stomach
churn together and make my head spin.

I find level and steady my legs.
A tall man moves out from the crowd.
His eyes search.
His brow questions.
Is he looking for me?

I paraphrase an old kid's book in my head.
Are you my father?

He's wearing a dark blue tailored suit, a red tie,
nice loafers with tassels.
Could he work for the National Security Agency?

Are you my father?

No. He passes me
and passionately kisses some woman on the lips.
Their PDA is totally embarrassing.
Get a room.

The crowd outside the station is
a whirling ball of sardines.
Taxi driver sharks
hover at the edge, watching,
then picking off people and leading them
into the jaws of their cabs.

A muscular man is peering around
in front of the crowd.

Are you my father?

His face is chiseled.

His buzz cut's gray.
His muscles are making his shirt
ripple with every movement.

I glance down at my own arms.
Yeah, I can see the DNA, sort of.

I'm pretty sure it's him.
His eyes are an eagle's on the hunt.
He looks through me as if to read my bone structure.

I smile and raise my hand to wave.
His stone face brakes into a smile.
He rushes forward, then curiously drops to one knee.
A little girl jumps into his arms.

I stop my idiotic wave
but continue my idiotic grin.

It's Emilia.
At least she's my excuse
for my wave and grin.
The woman with the suitcases
must be her mom.

"Have fun at Disneyland."

She doesn't answer me.
Instead I hear her say,
"Let's go, Uncle Bob,"
as the trio walks toward the parking lot.

I wander into the station.
The rank smell of cigarettes
and burnt coffee turns me around.

Just past some vending machines
slumps a slim, crooked man.
His brown hair is slicked-back with sweat.
A cigarette clings to his lower lip,
but he's not puffing.
The cigarette just hangs there,
smoldering,
dropping gray ashes on his shirt.
He's engrossed in his
Sports Illustrated.

I don't ask myself, *Are you my father?*
I sort of hope he isn't.

"Mr. Stout?"

He doesn't look up until my shadow
crosses his magazine.
He studies me for a bit,
looks at me with dark eyes over the top of his
sunglasses.

  "William?"

"Yes, sir."

   "You're bigger than I expected.
   Might not have recognized you,
   but I can't miss those eyes.
   They're just like your mom's."

Blue Pickup

His bright blue pickup is shiny,
the tires freshly Armor All'd.

I notice the airport parking permit
on the window
as I toss my duffel bag
in the truck bed.
At least he's telling the truth
about the airport job.

      "That all you brought?"

"It's all I got."

Truth.
It's pretty much all I have
in the entire world.
G'ma gave away
anything I outgrew
to the youth group
at church.

I left my shotgun and tactical knife with her.
She begged me to let her keep my sketches.

So I only brought a new pair of Chucks,
my hiking boots,
five T-shirts,
three pairs of jeans,
my phone,
socks, and underwear.

He slides over from the driver's side
and unlocks the door by hand.

I pull on the handle
and the smell of old oranges
and stale cigarette smoke
overpowers me.

The inside of the truck is filthy.
Plastic wrappers from cigarette packs,
crumpled-up receipts, cigarette ashes,
French fries, straws,
sesame seeds, and ketchup packs
are scattered everywhere.

I move a stack of mail from my seat.

     "Just toss 'em."

I drop the unopened mail on the floor.
He places his commuter cup
in a holder that hangs
from the air vent closest to the wheel.

"Um, thanks for letting me come."

     "Yeah. Well, no choice."

"G'ma wanted me to give you this."
I slide the small framed pic of Gramps
across the seat.

"I was hoping I'd see you at his service."

     "Had to work."

He glances at the picture
but doesn't pick it up.

From this direction
I see the family resemblance.
Not with me so much,
but his profile shares the same
edges and angles as Gramps'.

They also seem to share
the same sadness.
Maybe he was a soldier once.

Outside Inside

The line of old Spanish-style houses
ends abruptly.
A blinding shock of gold sunlight
makes me squint.
Then I see waves.
The blue expanse of the Pacific
sucks the air out of my lungs.

A group of hard bodies
are playing volleyball on the beach.
A slim bikini-clad blonde
dives for a ball.

Holy crap. She got it.
I crane my neck around.
Are all of these beach girls like her?

Barb Winslow was the hottest girl
in my old school, but there's no way
she could've dug that ball out,
let alone keep a bikini on.

Parked cars line the road on the right.
Guys my age are pulling on wet suits
behind their cars.
Surfboards are sticking out
the back or are lashed
to the roofs.

"Whoa," I say in my best Keanu Reeves.

"Don't get too excited.
You won't have much time
for any of that."

"Yes, sir."
What's up his ass?

My eyes are locked on the endless sand.
The waves beckon.
Pelicans fly in formation,
drafting each other like NASCAR racers.
I don't remember
ever seeing anything like this,
but I was born here.

Gray House

Expensive beachfront mansions
fade away,
replaced by older tract homes.

We park in the driveway
next to a gray stucco house.
One of a hundred gray stucco houses.
Nothing fancy, but not a dump.
The small lawn is tidy, but thin,
the fence straight.

He opens his door
and as he slides out,
the photo of Gramps
slips off the seat.
I lunge for it
just as he reaches for his cup.

Bonk! Forehead to forehead.

      "What kind of clumsy are you, boy?"

"Sorry."

I reach for the cup,
but he swats my hand. Hard.

      "Don't. Just get out."

I slide out the passenger door
but not before I see him
wipe off the picture of Gramps
and slip it into his pocket.

Just like his pickup,
the inside of his house
is sort of messy and scattered.
The stink of cigarettes and onions
permeates the place.

Is he the kind of man
who only cares
about appearances?
What other trash
might he be hiding?

The family room seems tiny.
Or maybe it's the huge recliner
that dominates the space.

Two small trash cans overflow
on either side of the chair—
a larger one with beer cans,
a smaller one with cigarette butts.

The chair faces a fifty-inch plasma TV.

He pushes me through the TV room
into the kitchen.

This is the source of the onion smell.
Dirty dishes are piled up in the sink.
A fly's paradise.

> "Bathroom," he says, pointing to a door.
> "I've made a bed for you in the back."

Two steps and we're in "my" room.
Before I can drop my bag, the house rules start.

The House Rules

"Now, William.
If you're going to stay here,
you have to follow my rules."

My bag hits the floor.

"Rule one.
The second floor is strictly off limits."

"Okay."
Wonder what sort of trash is up there.

"Rule two.
No friends over.
I don't want some kid
poking through my stuff."

"Yeah. Okay."
Not like I know anyone here.

"Rule three.
Don't fuck with the TV.
I don't want to see cartoons
or porn
or some reality show.
The TV is for sports."

I nod.
I'll miss *American Idol*?
That's fine with me.
I'd rather lose myself for hours in a book
than waste one minute watching TV.

"Rule four.
  I'm not paying for your Doritos,
  Monster drinks, or Internet.
  Get a job.
  Understand?"

I nod again.
He must be studying *Mein Kampf.*

  "That last one is important.
  I need to hear you say it, William."

"Yes, sir. I Understand."
Comandante Asshat.

  "Those are the conditions.
  Got it?"

"Yes, sir."
Shall I feed and water that beaten horse of yours?
Oh, wait.
It's dead.
Like, for days.

Bill or Dad

"You can call me Bill or Dad
if you want."

He waits.
My collar shrinks into a noose.
The corners of his mouth flinch down.
His eyebrow lifts ever so slightly.
He waits.

I swat at a pretend-fly buzzing past
in an attempt to break the tension.

He huffs.

Freeze-frame me.

I guess it wouldn't kill me to call him *Bill* or *Dad*.

But *Bill* feels wrong.
Too distant.
I guess we can be on a first-name basis,
but I generally save that
for a friend.

Dad is only a title.
And really, it's just a word
I can utter, but
I don't have to mean it.

All I can manage is,
"Yeah . . . okay."

In my defense,
at this point
he doesn't seem to be either
a *Bill* or a *Dad*.
I don't really know him.
He's just a guy
letting me sleep in his utility room.

He walks back into the kitchen
and pauses at the oven.
The oven door squeaks open,
then thumps closed.
His heavy footsteps clunk up the stairs
to the no-fly zone.

My Room

Six feet by ten feet
of unusable space.

Ragged black-and-white checkered linoleum floor.
A drain in the center.
Mouse traps in every corner.
White-washed cinder block walls.
A block-size window about shoulder high.
Hot outside.
Ice-cold inside.

Wedged between the dryer and the sink
that are older than dirt,
my bed is a camping cot
with an additional two-and-a-half inches
of "Open cell foam comfort."
At least that's what the tag reads.

The sink is a problem.
I'm either going to kick it
or hit my head on it,
depending on which way I decide to lie.

Three empty milk crates are stacked against the wall.
Starving student shelving.
I like them.

May as well unpack:
Shirts in the top crate.
Underwear and socks
in the bottom crate.
Toothbrush, toothpaste,
hairbrush, deodorant
in the middle crate.

My Chucks, boots, and gym bag
under the cot.
But where to put my photo
of Gramps and G'ma?
On the top crate for now.

The back door leads to
a small yard
with a shed.
No chicken coop,
like back in Kansas.

Moving across the country
shouldn't be this easy.
This is a big deal.
I left J-Bob, Kyle, Russell, Todd,
and the only home
I can remember.

What does it say about me
that I unpacked
in under five minutes?

I lie down on the cot.
Not bad for a camping bed.
The smell of the new mattress
makes me smile.
Like he actually went out
and got something just for me.

Ya know, I can't say I'm happy to be here.
Can't exactly say why I feel sort of depressed.

I guess that's how you feel when
you drop off the top shelf of anticipation
and land in the trash can of cruel reality.

My first day in Huntington Beach
with a dad who I haven't set eyes on
for years, and I'm spending it alone indoors.

Gramps used to say,
"You sleep in darkness
but live in the sunshine."
Gramps liked to be outside
in the fresh air,
in the sunlight.

It was like the sun was the
source of his power.

He didn't like it when I stayed indoors.
"Life is out there, William," he'd say.
"Way out there."

I sit up and slip on my hiking boots.
These things have seen a lot of miles
but still feel like they're just broken in.

Where do people hike here?

I unlock the deadbolt.
The back door
hasn't been opened
in a long time.

I have to pull hard.
The hinges scream,
but finally the door to my cell opens.
I'm so outta here.

Trash Bins

What little grass there is in the backyard
is either dead or on its way to dead.

The yard obviously hasn't seen much use in years.
The BBQ grill is rusted.
The propane tank is empty.

The shed is too small to be a garage
but too big to be just a tool shack.

A thick chain wraps around the shed doors
like a steel python.
A rusted padlock keeps it secure.
A peek through the dusty window reveals what looks like
metal pipes of some sort.

I find a gap in the back fence behind the shed.
I step through into a dusty unpaved alley.
Gray bins and blue bins line the alley behind each yard.

Gramps would often say,
"You can tell a lot about people
by the things they consider trash."

I peek inside "our" trash bins.
Lots of cans:
Spam, Bush's Baked Beans,
SpaghettiOs, and
those plastic chicken-shaped containers
from the grocery store,
filled with bones.

He smokes Winston Classics,
the red pack with the eagle on it.

The inside of the blue bin tells a familiar story:
Maker's Mark Kentucky Bourbon bottles.
A dead forest full of sports magazines:
ESPN, Sports Illustrated,
NFL, SLAM, and *Pro Football.*

So he's an old-school bachelor.
If he ever had a girlfriend,
she'd have made him eat better.
He might be a closet drunk
and sports is his porn.

I close the blue lid.
Across the alley,
a bushy brown dog is
watching me
with the most amazing
pale blue eyes.

"Hey, boy. Where'd you come from?
You lost?"
He sniffs at me, then trots away.

He's not wearing a collar.
The dog might be lost or a stray.
There's no one in sight,
so I follow him.

But I can't catch up to the dog.
At every turn
I catch a glimpse of his tail
as he trots up the next alley.

"Hey, boy. Stop!"
The dog pauses and looks back.
He studies me with his
pale eyes.

He has no injuries that I can see.
He seems well fed.
But he's timid.
No. He's wary,
like he's been abused maybe.

"Come here, boy."
I move a little closer.

His blue eyes study me with vigilance.

When I'm about ten feet away, I stop,
bend down, and hold out my hand.

"Good boy. Come here, boy."

He glances left, then right.
I can almost hear him thinking,
Should I let him pet me?

He takes a step toward me
but that's one step too close.
He spins on his back feet
and trots away.
I get up and follow him.

The alleys crisscross.
Maze-like.
Some stop abruptly.

Every time I slow,
the blue-eyed dog waits.
Not totally trusting me,
but asking me to keep following.

Bullies

"STOP!"

A little kid's voice?
I freeze in my tracks.

"Leave me alone!"

I try to orient on the cries.

The bushy brown dog
is just up ahead now,
looking back.
Is he waiting for me?

"Stop it!"

The kid screams again.
The dog darts around the corner.

I run after him.
The cries are coming from this direction.
I peek around the corner.
What the hell?

Three guys about my age
are surrounding a little kid
who looks maybe eight years old.

The bigger kids
are shoving the smaller kid,
stopping him from getting away.

Maybe they're acting out
some role-playing game?
Maybe the teens are
his older brothers?
Maybe it's none of my business?

The tallest guy has red hair.
Not natural red.
Red like in neon.

　　　"Shut up, Pussy."

Red shoves the little kid
so hard the kid falls over backward.

The frustration in my belly ignites.

"Hey!" I call out. "Hey, stop!"

Red turns and looks at me.
His expression is cool.
His eyes colder.

"Leave him alone!"

Red's cohorts step back,
but Red shakes his head.

　　　"Or what?
　　　Whatcha gonna do?"

The one heavyset guy looks worried.
The third guy with crazy green socks flips me off.
They return to their circle.

Red kicks at the kid
on the ground,
then yanks his backpack away.

"Can't you idiots hear?"

"We hear fine," Red mutters.

"Then why are you still here?"

"We'll go
when this is any of your business."

I move closer
so they can see
I outweigh them by thirty pounds.
Red finally steps away,
but I lose sight of him behind the other two.

Suddenly, a beer bottle smashes into the wall
next to my head.

"Fuck off!" says Green Socks.

Anger rushes hot up my neck.
The flames in my belly
blast rage out my eyes,
my nose, and my hands.

Before I realize it,
I'm at full sprint.

Another bottle whizzes past my head.

A Viking roar fills the air.
It takes a second to realize
the roar is coming from me.

The teens don't move fast enough.

Red fumbles with something in his pocket.
A knife flashes silver.

Gramps once told me,
"A killer never pulls a knife to scare you . . .
they just cut you when you least expect it."

I tackle Red before he can bring the knife down.
My shoulder smashes him just below his neck.
The knife skids across the asphalt.
We hit the ground.
I hear bone crack but it's not mine.

Red's screaming
like a banshee.
I give him one good punch
to the nose,
then feel more than see
someone coming at me.

I roll over just in time to avoid a kick to my ribs.
I spin and kick the feet out from under Green Socks.

Red scrambles away.
Green Socks rolls to his feet.
The heavyset guy is long gone.

The little kid's still on the ground
looking like a sheep.

"Go on," I tell him.
"Get outta here."

Too late.
Green Socks grabs the kid's backpack
and runs off.

He doesn't count on me following.
My hiking boots slow me down a little,
but I chase Green Socks from alley to alley.
Over fences, under stairways,
through hedges.

I follow him to a busy street.
He crosses while I wait for a car.
I race across to a driveway
where I saw him last.
It's a dead end.
There's just a Dumpster,
a few gates, and a tall fence.

But Green Socks has vanished.
I don't really care where or how.
I don't care
because he dropped the backpack
in the middle of the drive.

I examine the backpack.
There's a name tag:

Andy McKracken
1046 W. Corral Lane

Corral Lane

Finding my way back
to where I left the little kid
isn't easy.

All the roofs are tiled.
Entire neighborhoods are painted the same color.
All the trees are palm trees.

I walk facing backward
to see if anything looks familiar.
Nothing does.

I turn forward just in time to see
the bushy brown dog's tail
bobbing around a corner.

I jog after him,
Andy's backpack on my shoulder.
Again, the dog leads me through the maze.

I come to a street that opens into another
cookie-cutter neighborhood.
The street sign reads Corral Lane.
I start walking, looking for Andy's address,
but I don't have far to go.

Garlic Breath

"You should be ashamed."

"What?" I say to the woman
standing in her driveway.

She's got garlic breath,
jagged teeth, and
a heron's nest for hair.

"That's my son's backpack."

"You're Andy's mom?"
Poor kid.

Cocked head,
hands on hips,
one leg flexed.

The "Don't fuck with me or my kid" mom pose.

"Right."
I hand her the backpack.
"So is that your dog?"

"What dog?"

"The one with the blue eyes?"

"I don't know nothing 'bout any dog.
Now get going . . . Get outta here . . ."

"Lady, I wasn't the one who took Andy's backpack."

". . . before I call the cops."

"Ask him. Ask Andy."

She's not listening to me at all.
She stomps back into the house.

What a total bitch.
I've never met her before,
but something's familiar about her.

Her aggression gives me the chills.
The ocean air's cool, but I'm sweating
like I've run a marathon.

Did I forget to eat?
I'm shaking.

I go around to the back alley,
and lean against the fence.

Then I hear sniffling and whimpering.

First Contact

Soft crying.
From behind the wooden fence.

"Andy?"

Whimpers and sobs.
"Are you okay?
I gave your backpack to your mom."

        "Mom says not to talk."

The kid's hard to understand,
his words garbled between whimpers.

"Don't let those Zen Griefers
keep you down."

        "Zen Griefers do not like me.
        I am so dirty."

I lean in closer to the gap in the fence
to get a better look at the kid.

He has dark hair,
a red flannel shirt,
and cuffed jeans that are too long.
He's younger than I thought.

"You're not Andy."

"Not Andy. Patches."

He twists around and points
to the back of his head.
There's a squarish strip of blond-almost-white
in the middle of his dark brown hair.

"You need to go home again.
I don't belong here."

"You're an odd kid, Patches."

I turn away from the fence
and spy the bushy brown tail
at the end of the alley.

"I gotta go, Patches.
You gonna be okay?"

Patches' whimpering stops.
There's only silence.

"Patches?"

I look through the gap in the fence.
Patches is gone.

I jog around to the end of the alley,
but there's no sign of the dog.

First Night

A note on the kitchen table.

> Went to work.
> Food in the freezer.
> Don't forget. School tomorrow.

He didn't even ask where I was.
Did he notice I was gone?

Food.

Freezer.

Fish fillets.

Corn.

A box of taquitos . . .
with only one taquito.

Mystery brown stuff in a plastic bag.

Other mystery yellow stuff in a plastic bag.

Strawberries.

Pie crusts . . .
but no pies.

A mac and cheese meal.

Mac and cheese
cooking directions:
Microwave: nuke for seven minutes.
Oven: bake for twenty minutes,
or until golden brown.
I choose golden brown.

I open the oven
and find three bottles of Maker's Mark.

Gramps always said,
"Never touch a man's liquor or his licker."

Gramps had a raunchy sense of humor
mixed with a raunchy sort of wisdom.

Guess I'll use the microwave.

Recap

I gobble down the mac and cheese.
It's not golden or brown.
But it is hot
and cheesy.

Cheesy.

Kind of like my dad's note.
There's no "Glad you're here"
or "Welcome to your new home."
Just information.

Information.

Information was always lacking from my mom's cards.
For the last ten years or so,
I'd get one for Christmas
and one for my birthday.
Always about eleven days late.

> *Happy Holidays*
> *Mom*

> *Happy Birthday*
> *Mom*

Never any gift.
Never any return address.
Never any pictures.
Never anything about her life.
Never anything about my life.

Life.

Life here is starting on the wrong foot.
My first day and already a fight.
Red and his buddies aren't as bad
as the Edlebachers.
But maybe because of today,
they won't continue down that path.

Path.

My path?
I'm still hoping for the clouds to thin,
so I get some hint of my direction.
I don't know how long I get to live here.
I don't know if I even want to stay.

Stay.

Stay.
Come.
Sit.
Eat.
Don't go upstairs.
I'm not his son.
I'm his dog.

That dog.
His eyes are so blue.
I wish I could find that dog.

The Sink

Sleeping.

I dream.

A girl with cream-colored skin
caresses my shoulders.
We swim into the deepening blue sea.
I follow her down into a grotto.

She runs her hands down over my shoulders.
Her lips at my nipples, chest, stomach.
I close my eyes as her mouth takes me in.

I gasp.
But I can't get a breath.
There's no air down here in the darkness.
I thrash around.
Fight my way up to the light.

Briiiiiiing!

Bang!

My forehead smashes cold, hard ceramic.

Damn it!

Fucking sink!

First Day of School

Six more blocks to school.
All alone
walking.

I smell weed before
I see the
stoners.

Mini Mart is the
obvious
hangout.

Back home in Kansas
I would be
with them—

J-Bob, Kyle, Russell,
Todd, and me
smoking.

I want to be
on time.
Ready.

I want to be
the cool
new guy.

Clean, shiny cars
form a
long line.

In front of school
parents
drop off.

Spoiled kids wait
in the backseat,
ear buds in.

The line creeps forward
one car at
a time.

The older cool kids
jump out
and walk.

The younger nerds
wait 'til their
moms say.

I want to be the coolest.
My stomach
flutters.

Serpentine Girl

A girl walking just ahead.
Swaying.
Serpentine hips.
Swagger.
Graceful.

Nice long, flowing straight hair.
Sweeping.
Not quite a blonde,
not quite
brunette.

Sleek yet cool, casual style.
Except
for her knee-highs.
One green.
One white.

School Zone

School is loud.
Kids everywhere.

My old school was nothing like this.
There was no sense of urgency.
This place is like a small city.
There's even maps posted around the place.

There's no one central building
like my school back in Kansas.
Here, all the classrooms link together,
forming long lines
like spider legs from the admin building.
The main quad is at the center of the school
between the cafeteria and the admin building.
Everything's wide open.
Exposed.
Guess it never snows here.

I'm walking in slow motion.
The mass of kids swarm at light speed.
They greet each other with familiarity,
move to long-established meeting spots:
the flagpole, the bike racks,
tables in the main quad.

Seniors get their own parking lot here?
The lettermen
lean against their shiny cars.
They eye me.

The freshmen huddle together.
The boys in massive need of acne treatment.
The girls in massive need of better role models.

I follow Serpentine Girl
into the main office.
She must be a teacher's aide.
The staff all know her.
She flashes an electric smile.

I give my name to the school secretary
but miss hearing Serpentine Girl say hers.

I get a map and a printout with my daily schedule:

```
Counseling              Room 9
Phys Ed                 Gymnasium
Biology                 Room A127
Creative Writing        Room 219
Lunch
History                 Room A92
Statistics              Room 186
Art History             Room 31
```

When G'ma told my dad to sign me up for "Art,"
I was hoping for something
like sketching or painting—
not the *history* of it.
Dipwad.

Wait a second.
Before my first period
is *Counseling?*
WTF?

Room 9

A counselor? Me?
Before first period every day?

I dump my bag in my assigned locker,
follow the map,
and find Room 9.
I peek through the window.

Nerd Girl alert:
Pink-and-purple glasses.
Dark brown hair, major sheepdog bangs.
A flowery dress made from curtains.
Flats.
Bustling.
Arranging papers and files.

Nerd Girl opens the door.

> "William Stout?
> Come in."
> Have a seat.
> There's water in the pitcher."

I'm suddenly thirsty.
I fill the empty glass
next to the box of tissues.
I'm not gonna be crying.

"Any questions?"

"When do we start?"

"We already have."

"But don't we have to wait
for the counselor?"

"Sorry. I should've
introduced myself.
I'm Jill Archer.
Your counselor."

"But you're so young."

"I get that a lot."
She flips through a file.

Freeze-frame me.

She can't be much older than me.
But there's a diploma on the wall
with her name on it
from two years ago.
So the ink is still wet.

She studies me.
Watches me squirm.

"Young is relative.
I assure you
I am old enough to know my job."

"I wasn't questioning that."

"What are you questioning?"

"Why I have to be here."

"It's a requirement
for someone with your . . . history."

"You mean, my grandfather?"

"That and the conflicts at your last school."

"I was hoping all that was left back in Kansas."

"You might have left the conflicts behind,
but your history follows you."

Maybe it's this wooden chair,
maybe it's her age,
maybe it's what's written in that file,
but I can't seem to find a comfortable position.

"In here,
you can tell me anything
and there will be no judgment."

"That's good."

"Shall we start
with your grandfather's passing?"

"It wasn't a surprise."

"How so?"

"Cancer has a way of trumpeting its intentions."

"Were you two close?"

"I guess.
Gramps was cool.
He taught me to fish, shoot, and dance."

"Dance?
Like tap or what?"

"I don't know what it's called.
Like this . . ."

I have her interest.
There's something
in her face signaling
she is vulnerable.

I take her by the hands
pull her to her feet
and lead her in a slow rumba.

Red flushes up her neck
Embarrassment?
Or passion?

Doesn't matter.
Her reaction's telling.
She straightens up,
pushes away from me.

"Okay, no more of that. Sit."

I plop back into the uncomfortable chair.

"So how's living with your father?"

"Okay, I guess.
I've only been here a day."

"There's nothing in your file
about your mother.
Can you tell me about her?"

Freeze-frame me.

My mother?
My stomach quakes,
acid boils.
I force my sphincter to swallow the gas
back up inside my intestines.

"Um, she's . . . traveling."

"Vacation?"

"Work. She coordinates
the photo shoots
for *Sports Illustrated.*"

"Really? Sounds like an exciting job.
How'd she get into that line of work?"

"Well, she was one of the SI models.
Before."

Freeze-frame me.

I can't stop myself.
I've got no idea where I'm going with this.
But she seems to be buying
all the shit I'm shoveling.

My Mom

She's been a blonde,
a redhead,
and a stunning brunette.

She's worked in the White House,
as a contortionist in Las Vegas,
and once she was a war correspondent.

At least those were the stories
I told everyone back in Kansas.
I don't actually remember
what my mother looks like.

As long as I can remember,
my days started
with the sound of Gramps' chair
dragging across the linoleum,
followed by G'ma frying up cheesy eggs.

It's all a blank before that.

Locker Room

The locker room smells
of sweat, Axe, and ass.

Guys are checking a bulletin board
covered with Post-it notes.
One has my name and a number on it.
I'm locker twenty-seven—
middle row of five,
at the back wall.
Great.

Showers occupy the left side of the room.
Rows of lockers fill the right side
with a line of lockers against the wall
forming an L.

I have to pass through
the main gauntlet.
A band of naked gorillas
glaring, flexing, and posturing.

Establishing the
alpha, beta,
and dweeb.

They don't know me.
They wonder
where I fit
in their pecking order.

A tall, skinny, bright-eyed kid
watches me with curiosity.
He nudges the
athletic, hairless black kid
next to him.

They're open with their nakedness.
I keep my eyes above their necks.

They look like catalog models:
chiseled, slim,
and totally without body hair.

The tall one's eyes are jade green.
The black kid's are gold,
like they could melt the sun.

I'm not liking their interest.

The hairs on my arms rise,
and it's not from the temperature.

I bump into someone
solid, smooth, and warm.

    "Watch out, asshole."

A dark-haired kid
shoves me.

"Sorry."

    "Sorry you're an asshole."

I locate locker twenty-seven.
The combination's scrawled on the Post-it:
Right 34
Left 21
Right 3

It won't open.
I try again.

"Need help?" says Bright Eyes.

"This combination isn't right."

"Lemme see."

Something tells me I shouldn't,
but I'll look like a complete douche if I don't.
I hand him the Post-it.

"That's a seven, not a one.
Coach's handwriting isn't the best."

I try again with Left 27,
and the locker opens.
"Thanks."

"I'm Jim," says Bright Eyes.
"And this is Pete."
He points to the black kid
with the gold eyes.

"Hey. William."

I toss in my gym bag
and start to undress.

Bright-eyed Jim and Pete linger
too close and too long.

Dark Hair glares at me
as I slip out of my pants
and into the gym shorts
my dad bought me.

Banana Feet

I stand on the 27 painted on the asphalt.
There are thirty-eight kids in class.
Everyone's on their own number
a little more than arm's length apart.

Coach Harmon steps out
from the locker room.
He looks more like a hipster than
an athletic coach.
He hides his boyish face
with a dark brown beard.
He's fit but slim, not burly.

He starts at the kid on 1
and checks off attendance on his clipboard.

"Nice treads, Banana Feet."

Chuckling all around me.

"I'm talking to you, asshole."

I turn to see Dark Hair
smiling at me.
It's not a smile that says,
"I'm happy to see you."
It's more like the smile a coyote
gives to a bird
on the ground
with a broken wing.

"Nice treads, man.
They're very . . . yellow."

I look down at my new Chucks.
G'ma shopped all over town to find these.
I'd wanted brown ones,
but the only Chucks large enough
were bright yellow.

I'd hidden my disappointment
when she gave them to me . . .
but now I love these bright yellow Chucks.

"Careful, you might slip on those bananas."

More chuckling.

Coach gives a look to Dark Hair.

"Needlemier, knock it off.
You new, Stout?"

"Yes, sir."

"Sir? You certainly can't be from around here.
Come with me.
Everyone else, push-ups."

Groans.

Gift

Coach leads me to his office.
Less ass smell, but lots more sweat.

"You've got big feet."
"Yeah."

"Shoe size?"

"Twelve maybe?"

"Lift."

He raises his foot up to mine.

"Wait here."

He heads into a back room,
leaving me staring at his old desk
and some pictures on the wall.

I look closer.
The pics are all of the same
college running back.

"Here.
These should fit you."

Coach hands me a box of new running shoes.

"Thanks, but I can't."

"I'll give them to you
for the same price I paid."

"But I've got no money."

"That's okay. I got them for free."

"Thanks. But why?"

"You're new.
You've got three days
before you get a nickname or a reputation.
'Banana Feet' isn't a great way
to start your school year."

Wind Sprints

I get back to number 27
with my new shoes.

Needlemier glances over, disappointed.

> "Okay, ladies," Coach growls.
> "Sprints."

More groans.

> "To the posts and back."

We take off,
a flock of ostriches,
all legs
and dust.

The new shoes are light.
I run at seventy percent.
Don't want to stand out.

It's two football fields to the goalposts.

Needlemier shoves me.
I stumble, but stay upright.
Asswipe.

Flames in my belly.
Heat rises up my neck.
I chase him.
He cuts around the goalpost.

I pick up the pace, but he's back
before I can catch him.

The rest of the class jogs in behind us.

"I said sprints, not jogs,"
Coach growls.
"Again, and this time
run 'til you piss blood."

We go again.
This time I see Needlemier coming.

I wait 'til he's next to me.
His weight shifts,
readying to shoulder me.
So I stop.
He plunges in front of me,
stumbles, but keeps going.

Needlemier picks up his pace.
We get to the posts.
He darts just ahead of me.

I grab the post, whip myself around,
and race up behind him.
His breathing's rough,
gasps more than breaths.

A ten-yard gap,
but that's all the rope I'll give him.
I've got more.
I sprint hard
and pass him.
No. I demolish him.

I'm first back.
I pant.
Beads of sweat on my brow.

Needlemier staggers in behind me
and doubles over.
His chest heaves.
He might toss.

> "Nice run, Banana Feet,"
> Needlemier gasps.

> "Might have to change that to 'Flash,'"
> Coach says.

I look from Needlemier to Coach.
"Must be the shoes."

Biology

This classroom's weird.
There are no individual desks.
Instead there are tall lab tables
with three or four chairs at each of them.

"Form teams for your lab work,"
the teacher says.

There's a couple of empty chairs
at the back,
but the jocks are saving them.

The only free chair I can find
is next to a plump kid slouching
over his iPad.
Every few seconds he pushes
his Coke-bottle glasses
up the bridge of his nose.

The kid glances up at me,
then flinches as if I've thrown a punch.
By the looks of him,
he's been conditioned.

I'm just about to call this class loser,
when the door opens.
Angels sing.
In saunters
Serpentine Girl.

Her hair swings back and forth with every step,
like a whip cracking.
Her jeggings reveal every muscle and curve.

Her skin's like cream with a hint of coffee.
Her eyes are an interesting color—
not blue
not green
not brown,
but all three depending on how you look at her.

Wait.
Freeze my heart.

Did she just look at me?
Was that a smile?
I mean, it wasn't all teeth,
but the corner of her lips raised,
I'm almost sure.

Heart reengage.

Oh, no.
One of those open chairs at the back?
The jocks were saving it for her.
Is one of those meatheads her boyfriend?
Does it matter?

I glance back.
Meathead One is all over her.
He's leaning in.
She's pushing him away,
not like rejection,
more like his breath stinks.

She laughs and jokes with the others.
She's got a nice way about her.
Not flirty.

Engaging.

The teacher begins the roll call.

> "Benn."

> "Here."

He reads off more names,
receives more "here"s.

> "Goligowski."

> "Right here, Mr. Lipston,"
> Coke-bottle eyes chirps.

> "Helliberg?"

> "I'm here."

It's Serpentine Girl.

Her voice is sweet,
with a hint of something.
An accent maybe.

I glance over my shoulder,
then snap my head forward.

She's looking at me!

I'm curious about her.
I hope she's curious about me.

I pretend to drop my pencil
and look back over my shoulder.
For sure she's looking at me.

She looks up every time I look at her.
No one else seems to notice me,
and yet she's noticing every move I make.

But she doesn't look at me with recognition.
It's like she's studying me.
No.
It's like she's reading me.

Her eyes shine.
She's got a real smile this time.
I smile back.

She cocks her head,
gives me a quizzical look.
What does she want to know?
She points toward the front of the class.

I turn around.

"Stout? William Stout?"

"Oh. Yeah.
That's me."

Giggles from everyone.
I glance around.
All eyes are looking at me.
A quick look back at her.
The meathead's glaring.

Freeze-frame me.

Great way to make a first impression.

I totally look like a dork
who doesn't even know his own name
when it's said out loud.

Red heat rises to my cheeks.

At least she notices me.

I take a chance
and glance back over my shoulder.
She glances up at me and smiles.
I don't believe she thinks I'm an idiot.

Mr. Lipston begins
his first-day speech:

> "We're going to study
> the human anatomy
> from top to bottom."

I open my textbook to the first chapter.

The first slide is a diagram
of the human eye.

Shasten

The bell rings.

It's a mad rush out the door.
Kids scatter in all directions.
I step aside to avoid the current.

> "I'm Ollie."

I turn toward the squeaky voice.
It's Coke-bottle eyes.
"I'm William."

> "If you want to study together,
> I'm free most afternoons."

"Thanks for the offer."

> "I figured since we're going to be
> sitting next to each other all year—"

"Right. Let's see how it goes."

> "Oh. Okay. See you tomorrow?"

"Yup."

> "Looks like you have new friend,"
> says a sweet voice behind me.

Serpentine Girl.

"Huh? Yeah. Gotta start somewhere."

> "Welcome to Marina High.
> I'm Shasten."

That sweet voice again.
It tickles my ears.

"I'm . . ."

> "Stout? William Stout?"
> snarks one of the meatheads.
> "We all know your name
> even if you don't."

I bristle.
My hands clench to fists.
Maybe it's instinct.
Territory or testosterone;
contest or competition.
I can't help myself.

> "Be nice, Bender,"
> Shasten says.

"Bender? Your name's Bender?"

> "Yeah. Why? You think it's funny?"

"Oh, no. I just repeat things so I'll remember them."

Bender pauses.
Shasten giggles.

> "Funny. That's pretty funny,"
> Bender says.

Shasten slows.
Bender the meathead moves down the hallway.

   "So is it William or Will?"

"William.
Will can lead to Willie
and no one wants to be called one of those."

   "Why? What's a Willie?"

My cheeks are hot again.
What do I say now?
I can't tell her a Willie
is another name for a penis.

"It's nothing—"

   "I'm kidding.
   I *know* what a Willie is."

Hold on.
She's fucking with me?
That's actually cool.
Really cool.

"I guess it's my fault for bringing it up."

   "It was worth it.
   I like that shade of red
   on your face.

"So where'd you move from?"

"Kansas."

"With Dorothy and Toto too?"

"Yeah. Now I live with the Tin Man."

Her smile completely disorients me.
I almost walk into a post.

"And you're from where?"

"I was born in a place where
Pippi Longstocking is Queen,
hockey players are heroes,
and reindeer rule."

"Wyoming?"

"No, silly. Sweden."

"That explains the accent."

"Do I still have one?
Even after four years?
I'll have to work harder."

"Please don't. I like it."

She smiles again.
I like that too,
but I can't tell her that.

"Are you following me?"

"No. Just going to my next class."

"Which is where, William?"

"Creative Writing. Room 219."

"Then you *are* following me."

"No. What makes you say that?"

"Room 219 is back that way."

She points behind us.
I'm red again,
but this time I don't mind.
It feels right.

Creative Writing

The Creative Writing teacher,
Mrs. Long, is really cool.
She's some sort of author
when she's not teaching.
She seems young,
but her hair's completely white.

I'm stumped by the first exercise.
She wants us to answer the question,
"What is the most important thing
I should know about you?"

I have no idea what to write.
I could write that I'd like her to know
that I'm new here,
but that's not very important.

I could write that the most important
thing she should know about me
is that I have to work hard
to have a friendly exterior.

Inside I'm pissed.
Pissed that I don't remember my mother.
Pissed at my father for being absent.
Pissed that Gramps died.

The clock's ticking toward noon.
I start writing furiously.

The bell rings.
I hand in my essay titled,
"I'm New Here."

Ollie

Lunchtime. Ergh.

I know about five people here now,
but I only want to sit with one of them.
I pretend to be on my phone
while I scan the lunch crowd.

The cafeteria's for
the sophomores and juniors.
Seniors hold court outside.

I don't see Shasten anywhere,
but I do see Needlemier at the tables
in the main quad.

I should've guessed
he'd be sitting with Bender.
They're not asking me to join them,
so I just stay on my pretend phone call.

There's a tree between the admin offices
and the parking lot.
Seems quiet.

I reach the tree.
There's someone already sitting
on the grass.
I step back.
Too late.

> "Come join me.
> There's plenty of room."

Ollie Goligowski looks up
from under the shade of the tree.
His Coke-bottle glasses magnify
his eyes to the size of tennis balls.
Tennis balls filled with loneliness.

Freeze-frame me.

What to do?
I'll probably be sitting
with this kid the rest of the year.
I might even study with him,
if he turns out to be smart.

In class, you're forced to be together.
Outside class? You're tagging yourself.

What if people see us
having lunch together?

Ollie's eyes reduce to normal size.
His smile
reduces from high beam
to daytime running lights.

Crap. Why do I care
what people think?

"Thanks, Ollie."
I plop down next to him.

His smile goes back to high beam.

"I have three questions for you."

"Okay.
I just moved from Kansas.
I was born here.
I live with my dad."

      "Nice to know,
      but not the questions
      I was going to ask."

"Oh. Okay then, shoot."

      "What's your biggest regret?"

"Biggest regret? Hmmm.
I guess not telling Gramps—
my grandfather—
I loved him."

      "And your biggest triumph?"

"Beating the rap on my
aggravated assault case."

      "You're kidding right?"

"Oh, yeah. Joke."

I'm not kidding.
But I don't need anyone
to know about my past.
I gotta be more careful.

"I guess my triumphs have been small."

"Well, you moved here.
That's a triumph."

"Sure is."
Jury's still out on that one.
"That's two questions.
What's your third?"

"This one's a toughie."

"I'm ready."
I brace myself.

"Football.
European or American?"

"Um . . . that actually *is* tough,
but I'll go with American
to prove I'm patriotic."

"I'm gonna ask you these again."

"But I just answered them."

"I'm hoping your answers
will change
by the end of the year."

"You're quite a deep thinker, Ollie."

"I like to believe so."

Ollie's not at all what I expected.

I munch on my SPAM, mustard,
and mayo sandwich.

> "What *is* that?"
> Ollie sounds disgusted.

"SPAM.
The only thing I've found
at my father's house
that resembles meat."

> "You don't look Hawaiian."

"Nope, not that I know of."

> "Is your father a survivalist?"

"No. Why?"

> "SPAM is sort of a
> delicacy in Hawaii.
> Survivalists are fond of canned
> products with long shelf lives."

"Well, he's not one of those.
He works for the NSA.
Spy stuff."

> "My dad's a forensic scientist.
> So he sits on a stool and looks at a stool."

"Ha, ha. That's a cool job, though."

"Not as cool as my mom's.
She's a professional odor tester."

"What the hell is that?"

"She sniffs people's armpits."

"There's no such job."

"No, really.
She's paid by some
deodorant company
to sniff armpits
before, then after,
they put on deodorant."

"You're fucking with me, Ollie."

Ollie's looking past me
with his tennis ball eyes.
I follow his gaze.

Holy shit.
Shasten's coming right toward us.

I want to jump up and run,
or maybe punch Ollie.
Anything but look like we're friends.

"Hi, William. Ollie."

"Aaaah," is all that Ollie can muster.

"Shasten. Um, we were just . . ."

"Having lunch I see."

"Hey, there's my girl."
Needlemier's here all of sudden,
slipping his arm around Shasten's waist.

No f'ing way.
Needlemier?
Of all the asswipes in the world,
he's her boyfriend?

"Bradley,
this is William.
He's new here."

"We've met,"
Needlemier grunts.

Shasten sideslips Needlemier's arm.
It's not a solid rebuff, but it gives me hope.

"What are you looking at, googly eyes?"
Needlemier spits at Ollie.

Ollie shakes his head.
"Nothing."

I stand up.
I don't know why.

Ollie's the sort of kid
I'd have picked on back in Kansas.
But that was before our Q and A session.
Now I feel like I gotta protect him.

I gesture to Ollie behind my back.
He gets the hint and packs up his lunch.

"So Needlemier, what's your deal?"

    "My deal?"

"Ya know? Your story?"

Out of the corner of my eye,
I see Ollie,
like a cloud on a breeze,
move slowly away.

Needlemier squares off with me.
He glances from my face to my chest,
to my arms, and then my shoulders,
but he doesn't bring himself to lock eyes with me.

I've won already.
He's forgotten all about Ollie.

"I'm the captain of the varsity football team.
What's *your* deal?"

"Who, me?
I'm Batman."

Giggles from Shasten.

> "If you two are done
> pissing on trees,
> class is about to start."

They walk off side by side.

Just as I'm about to turn,
Shasten tosses a look
over her shoulder.
She screws up her face
and rolls her eyes.
I'm hoping this means
she knows
he's an asswipe.

Blank Slate

"History is the study of past
acts, events, and ideas
that can or will shape the course
of the future," Mrs. Chen says,
passing out the syllabus.
"History is what roots you
to your family,
to your community,
and to your world."

I don't have any history
with these people.
What does that say about
the course of my future?

I don't feel very rooted
to anyone or anything.

But maybe that's a blessing.

Being new,
without history,
without links,
and without relationships,
I'm free to shed
the rougher spots of my skin,
those blotches and scars
that become the target of
unspoken questions:

Where are his real parents?
What happened?
Will the rough hand
of life deform him?

Here, at least
for the time being,
I am free.

Free to display my shinier points.
Free to take on a fresh persona.
Free to actually become
the person I pretend to be.

Day's End

After Stats (boring!),
I bounce over to Art History,
although I have no clue where it is.

Ollie comes up to me
as I search the hallways.

> "Thanks for
> what you did
> at lunch."

"No worries."

> "Nice to have someone
> watching out for me."

I hope he's not expecting me
to be his bodyguard.

I finally find Room 31.

I think Art History's going to be okay.
Mr. Perry's cool, although
he seems obsessed
with Impressionism.
Like all of them: Pre, during, and Post.

Mary Cassatt's stuff makes me
want to puke.
Mothers, babies and girls—
they seem posed.
Unreal.
The SPAM's threatening to rise.

Gauguin spent a lot of time
painting sleeping
chubby women.
At least there aren't any babies.

Van Gogh's early work
is so different
than his later stuff.

Munch. Edvard f'ing Munch.
His stuff speaks my language:

The Scream, Agony, Vampire.
Oh my freaking God,
this guy was dark and possibly
suffering from extreme melancholy.

I dig sketching dark things.
My anthology of famous crime scenes
was "very provocative,"
according to my old school.

G'ma wouldn't let me
bring those sketches with me.
I'm not sure if she liked them
or just didn't want
anyone else to see
what goes on inside my head.

If these people can sell for big bucks,
who knows?
Maybe I can become a famous artist.

The bell rings and school's done.

I get to my locker.
I've totally memorized
the combination already.
I shove books in my backpack
and head for my dad's house.
I feel like a grunt in the army.
My pack must weigh at least fifty pounds.

It's a mega clusterfuck
in the parking lot.
Cars are stuck in a
slow-motion
Candy Crush Saga.

Glad I'm walking . . .
well, except for the backpack.

My Dad's House – Day Two

I get to my dad's place
and find another note
on the fridge:

> Watching the game at Legends.
> There's leftovers.
> Don't forget the house rules.

Right.
No upstairs.
No friends over.
No TV.
And get a job.

The first three are easy.
The fourth's gonna take some effort.

I quickly hammer out
most of my homework
while I chow down
the rest of the mac and cheese.

My Creative Writing assignment
is sort of weird.
Mrs. Long wants us to find a location
that we're inspired by,
take a picture,
then write a short story about it.

I look around the kitchen,
then in my room.

The only thing even slightly inspiring
is the old sink.
It inspires me to pull it out of the wall.
But that might not make such a good story.

I've got hours of daylight left.
As Gramps would say,
"Move that ass before
the night catches you."

Might as well explore the town.
Maybe walk down the beach.
That might be inspiring.

Maybe along the way
I can see what sort of places
might be cool to work at.

Shut Doors

Gramps used to say,
"Gotta respect counter people.
Sure, they might be
uneducated gatekeepers,
but you know what?
Clerks run the world."

Eddie's Diner—
a burger joint
in an Airstream.

"What can I get you?"

"Do you have any openings?"
I ask the waitress.

"No."

Before I can ask her for suggestions,
she's back behind the counter
pouring coffee and refilling sodas.

Hoobie's Surf Shoppe—
board shorts, flip-flops,
wet suits,
all kinds of surfboards,
and girls.

Not just any girls.
Golden-skinned-
drenched-in-the-sun-
like-Dip-Cones
girls.

Working here would be totally awesome.

I wander toward the group
of golden girls
like a zombie hungry for girl brains.

Two of the girls glance in my direction.
I quickly look away and
finger clothes on a rack,
then suddenly realize
I'm holding a blue bikini.

Giggles.

The heat on my cheeks
is so extreme I swear
my hair's gonna singe.

I move over to the surfboards.
Long boards,
wood boards,
foam boards,
and short, pointy tip boards,
all lined up like cocks.

I love this place.

>   "Hey, man."
>   A blond dreadhead
>   nods at me.
>   "Trestles or 17th Street?"

"What?"

"Where do you surf?"

"Oh, I'm new here."

"I gotcha.
Help you with anything?"

"Curious if you have any job openings."

"Maybe. Follow me."

Dreadhead shuffles toward
the back of the store.
We pass all sorts of cool surf gear.
He leads me to tall guy in a straw hat
whose skin looks like the bark of a tree,
weathered, brown,
but he's not a man of color.

"Here's the main dude
with all the answers.
Barney here's looking for a gig."

"Not Barney. I'm William."

"He means you're not from here."

"Oh. Right. Joke."

Dreadhead shuffles away.

"I'm Jack Hoobie.
You surf?"

Freeze-frame me.

How do I answer?

If I tell the truth,
I won't get the job.
If I lie,
I might drown
in the churning riptide
of untruths.

But omission isn't really telling a lie.
Omission tilts the truth.
It might suggest an impression.
Omission often creates a vacuum of facts
that leads to an unvalidated conclusion.
And besides, it's not on me
what he chooses to believe.

"I was born here,
so I've got seawater in my blood."

    "Me too."

"I'm just back after a few years,
so I haven't figured out the local scene yet.
17th Street or Trestles. Ya know?"

    "Gotcha."

He hands me an application.
I read through it, but
I don't know half the terms in the questions.

Like what's a Bonzer,
and how is it similar
to a single-to-double board?

What's the difference between
a long, short, wood, or foam board?

Do I ever use a boogie, body,
or skim board?

I write in my name, address, and
cell number, and
hand the form back to him.

Jack frowns at my application.

"We'll give you a call
if a gig opens up."

Something in his tone says
he won't be calling anytime soon.

"Mind if I take some pics for a school project?"

"Radical, dude."

My Eyes

My frown
almost cuts my face in half.

My feet
stomp the sidewalk.

My mind
can't solve House Rule 4.

My head
spins with the impossibilities.

My eyes
catch a glimpse of a kid.

He stands
in the middle of the road.

Red shirt.
His pant legs are rolled up.

It's Patches.
"Hey, Patches!" I call.

"Look out!"
A car's coming up the street.

The driver
doesn't slow down.

"Asshole!"
I'm yelling as I cross the street.

Patches turns
and runs up a driveway.

Where in the fuck
are this kid's parents?

I wouldn't leave a dog outside alone.
How can I leave a kid?

But where is he now?
I swear he was just in front of me.

There's no sign of him
in the front yard.

I search the side of the house,
then move around to the back

just in time to see his little feet
vanish through the doggie door.

Someone Else's House

I get down
on all fours
and poke my head
through the doggie door.

"Hey,
come back,"
I whisper.
Giggles from somewhere inside.
"This isn't your house."

Thumps,
footfalls,
something big
crashes, more giggles.

I can't slip
my shoulders
through the narrow
doggie door threshold.

But
can I
stretch one arm
up to maybe
unlock the deadbolt?

Yes!
I'm in!
What the hell's his deal?
I search the hall.
Where's he hiding?

Chaos

I get to the living
room and freeze.

The room's totally trashed.
A sofa's sideways.
A lounge chair's upside down.
Books scattered all over the floor.

How could a little kid
wreak havoc so fast?

If I clean it up,
the owners might not know
anyone's been here.
All I know is that
I can't leave it this way.
I upright the lounge chair,
move the sofa back,
pile books onto the shelves.

There's a thump in the next room.

"Patches?"

I enter what looks like a library.
A huge desk dominates one wall.
A tall cabinet dominates the other.
Bookshelves between.
The cabinet door moves.

"Patches? You in there?"

I yank open the cabinet door.
No Patches.
Just guns.
Lots of guns.

Shotguns.
Semi-auto pistols.
A scoped hunting rifle.
Every gun has a label under it
with a description.

Someone's running,
then a door slams.
Little kid giggles.

I leap into the hallway
and follow the giggles
to a closed door.

I try the knob
but it's locked from
the inside.

"Patches? Come out of there."

> "You sound like Mommy
> When I have been a bad boy.
> She doesn't like me."

"I'm sure your mommy likes you fine.
She probably loves you a bunch.
But I'm also sure when you do things like this,
it's gonna make people crazy.
Now, unlock the door."

"When Mommy loves me,
She makes me take off my pants.
She sucks my pee-pee.

She gives me away.
The men make me kiss their mouth.
They hurt my bottom."

What the fuck!?

"What did you just say?"

Something threatens to climb out of my throat.
I gag.
My stomach pitches.

The hallway's constricting me
like a snake.
I crumple against the wall.
I breathe deep and slow.
What's just happened?

There's rustling
behind the door.

"Patches, unlock the door.
Now!"

I press my shoulder against the door,
wrench the knob.
It finally pops open.

It's the bathroom.

I search behind
the shower curtain,
under the sink.
But Patches has vanished again.

And then, through the open window,
I see him running out to the sidewalk
just as a Volvo station wagon begins
to turn into the driveway.

I hope I got things cleaned up enough
in the other room,
but I can't worry about that now.

I squeeze through the bathroom window
and drop to the ground
behind some hedges.

The car drives past me.
I run to the sidewalk
and search the street with my eyes.

There's no sign of Patches.

> "You lose something?"
> an older woman asks
> as she gets out of the Volvo.

"Yeah, a little kid.
Maybe you know him?
His name's Patches."

"Sorry, don't know any kids
by that name."

She pulls her mail from the mailbox,
but keeps her eyes on me.

"You're a bit old
for Hide-and-Seek,
aren't you?"

"What? Oh, yeah,
probably, but it's still fun."

I head down the street
in the direction where
I last saw Patches.

The weight of the
old woman's stare
is heavy on my back.

I need to find him.
See if he's telling the truth.

If he's not,
I'll be so pissed.

And if he is,
I need to save him.

Misspellings

To my surprise,
my father's home
and he's cooking.
Something that actually smells good.

"Hi . . . um."

      "Where you been?"

"Looking for a job."

      "Good. Any bites?"

"Nothing concrete."

His lower lip
purses out in a pout.

"But the guy at the surf shop
said he'd call if something opens up."

His lower lip
sucks back in.

      "Well, it's not easy
      getting a job these days.
      So don't give up."

I nod.
      "Hungry?"

"Starving."

Actually I wasn't all that hungry
until he asked.
My encounter with Patches
drained me,
left me shaken.
Now I need to fill
the empty space.

He sets two steaming plates on the table.

"Chicken Alfredo."

I sit at the table.
Gramps would've said grace.
G'ma would've just raised her fork
to signal it was okay to start eating.
I've got no idea of my dad's ritual.

I put my hands together
and bow my head.

"You don't have to do that here."

I lift my head,
my hands still in prayer.

"In fact, I'd rather you don't."

So he's not religious
like Gramps.
How is that possible?

"I'm sure my dad ingrained
that crap into your head
like he did with me, but
prayer doesn't seem to work here."
He waves at me.
"Go on.
Eat before it gets cold."

Something bad must've happened
to make him question his faith.
I wonder what.

I power down some dinner.

"This is great.
Can you teach me
how to make it?"

      "Yeah, it's really easy.
      You boil water,
      toss in the noodles,
      nuke the sauce."

"That *is* easy."
And probably why it tastes good.
"Were you not working today?"

      "No, I am,
      just starting on
      the night shift this week."

"I didn't know the NSA
had a second shift."

"TSA. Not NSA."

"TSA?
But Gramps said NSA."

"He also spelled *Kansas* with a z."

"Yeah.
His spelling really did suck.
So you don't carry a gun?"

"Nope. I carry luggage."

"What?"

"Yup, I'm one of the unseen heroes,
slogging checked luggage
to and from the scanners.
Sorry to disappoint you."

"No, I'm not.
I'm sort of glad.
Don't have to worry
about you getting killed."

"Only if a suitcase explodes."

I'm being nice.
I don't worry about him getting killed
and I *am* kind of disappointed.

"National Security"
versus
"Transportation Security."
The first one just sounds cooler.
Like he's a spy or something.

Now, he just sounds
like a glorified porter.

Then it hits me.
If he only works
for the TSA,
then why couldn't he
come for Gramps'
funeral?

Why didn't he ever
visit me
in Kansas?

Why didn't
he take me
sooner?

What a dickwad.

Dinner finishes
without any more
conversation.

He leaves for work.
I do the dishes.

I want to search Facebook
for Shasten,
but my pre-paid minutes are running low.

I go to bed early
so I can get to tomorrow
sooner.

Before I close my eyes,
I say a short prayer
for Patches.
I hope he's dreaming
of candy,
toys,
and ice cream.
I wish him lots of laughter.
I pray he's safe.

My Toe

Sleeping.

A beautiful girl with luxurious long blond hair
runs her hands down over my shoulders.
Her lips at my nipples, chest, stomach.
I close my eyes as her mouth takes me in.

I gasp at the sensation of her tongue
on the tip of my cock.
The warmth,
the wet,
the wonderment.

She wraps her arms around me.
Her skin is soft against mine.
Her arms grow longer, stronger,
lengthening into tentacles
with disk-shaped suckers.

The suckers bite into my flesh
as the tentacles constrict.

I can't get a breath.
I can't move.

The suckers bite at my chest,
at my arms,
at my thighs.

They seem to be searching for my balls.
I get my right leg free.

I kick hard.

Briiiiiiing!

Bang!

My big toe smashes
into the cold hard ceramic.

Damn it!

Fucking sink again!

Not Hunting

How long will I have
to go to counseling?
Will she give me a pass once
she thinks I'm not some raging maniac
hell-bent on killing everyone?
Or is this a mandatory year-long thing?

Her door is open,
so I go ahead and sit
in the uncomfortable wooden chair.

Jill Archer sits in front of me.

> "So yesterday you mentioned your
> grandfather taught you
> to dance and shoot."

"Right."

> "But you didn't say *hunt.*
> Why not?"

"No hunting.
Not like deer or anything."

> "So what would you shoot?"

"Cantaloupes."

> "Cantaloupe?"

"Frozen ones"

> "Like, melons?"

"Gramps was a sniper
during the last years of Vietnam.
He taught me to shoot from long distance."

"Okay, but why frozen cantaloupe?"

"Because a melon explodes
like a human head."

"Oh. Um. I would never have thought . . . that."

"Shooting guns is not as easy
as it looks on TV or in the movies."

I shape my right hand like a gun,
then lift my left arm in line
like I'm holding a rifle stock.
I lower my head to a sighting position.

"You need to get a good cheek weld.
But most important is your breathing."

"You don't just hold your breath
and pull the trigger?"

"No. You squeeze on the downbeat."

"Sounds like reggae."

"It is, kind of.
See, you have to take
three deep breaths.
In through your nose,
out through your mouth.
Slows your heart rate."

"That makes sense."

"On the third exhale,
between breaths,
you squeeze the trigger straight back,
on the downbeat."

"You know, I have to admit
when you first said your grandfather
was a sniper, I wanted to call bullshit."

I can't help but giggle
at her use of profanity.
It comes out of her mouth
like a badly spoken foreign language.

"But I can see by your description
that he must've known his stuff."

"He must have.
He made it through four
tours."

"Squeeze on the downbeat.
I'll remember that."

Gramps used to say,
"You live
or die
between breaths."

Yellow Flags

I stand on 27.
Before Needlemier can begin his cawing,
Coach splits our class into two groups:
the Reds and the Yellows.

"Flag football today."

Needlemier beams.
Coach tosses belts at us.
We attach colored flags on either side
of our waists with Velcro.

The Reds consist of Needlemier
and all his muscle-bound meathead friends.

The Yellows are me, Jim, Pete,
and the smallest kids in class.

> "Hey, Coach?" Jim says.
> "Is it me, or do the teams seem lopsided?"

> "This is an exercise in teamwork,
> in the guise of a football game."

> "Looks more like suicide,"
> Pete mutters.

> "What do you think, Flash?"
> Coach looks at me.

"Well, we Yellows are probably smarter."

Coach nods.

"What else do you have on your side?"

Is Coach expecting an answer
or is he giving me a hint?

We shuffle onto the field.

"So if I remember correctly, Jim,
you and Pete came in
just behind me at
yesterday's wind sprints."

"Yeah? So?"

"So I think Coach
split the teams
this way on purpose.
We might be smaller,
but we're definitely faster."

Jim looks over at the Reds.

"Way faster, all except Needlemier."

"And he'll quarterback."

"What makes you say that?"

"His ego."

Coach has us kick off.
A short floppy-haired kid
sets the football up.

"Salcido plays soccer,"
Jim says.

"Keep it away
from Needlemier, Salcido!"

Boom.
Salcido has one hell of a leg
and gets his foot all into it.
It's high and to the left.

The Reds make a line
in front of their runner.
Our small guys can't penetrate.

I go left and cut inside.
Their runner is fast,
but I get a hand on his hip
and rip off his flag.

Just as I predicted,
Needlemier is quarterback.

Jim and Pete pick their guys to cover.

I guess I'll be rover.

"Red Dog two, hut, hut, hut!"
Needlemier barks.

They go in motion.
Our line's so small, they get
bowled over backward.

Needlemier has time and throws
a heat-seeking missile downfield.

Jim's fast and saves a touchdown.
But we still can't stop them.

The game goes on;
we trail twenty-one to zip.

      "Two minutes!"

We have the ball at our twenty.
Pete has a good arm,
but Needlemier's covering me tight
and I can't get free.

Last huddle.

      "Hand off to William,"
      Pete suggests.

      "I can get free,"
      Jim says.

      "They're not giving me
      any time to pass,"
      Pete says.

"How 'bout a reverse?"

Pete and Jim nod.

We break the huddle.

I line up wide.
Salcido snaps the ball.
Pete fakes a pass to Jim.

I reverse.

Pete hands the ball to me.

Needlemier races to intercept me at the line.
His meatheads have our guys on the ground.

Jim's racing down the side
and he's all alone.

I set my back foot
and launch a Hail Mary
with all my weight.

The ball tracks straight,
but flies over Jim's head
by ten yards.

Game over.
We head for the showers.

"Good game, guys."

"We didn't even score, Coach."

"No, but you didn't give up.
And that last pass of yours
was almost sixty yards."

"I overthrew him."

"Next time he'll know
not to stop running."

"Maybe next time,
you won't stack the odds
against us."

"Look, Flash,
it's not always about points
or being the hero.
Sometimes it's simply
a test of character.
How you face the odds.
How you find solutions.
How you handle the heat."

Coach pats me on the shoulder.

"So, like I said before,
good game."

Shower Seen

Damn, I really wanted to beat
Needlemier and his meatheads,
but all I did was sweat.
I need to shower.

Don't want to stink
when I see Shasten
in Bio.

I strip off my sweaty clothes,
grab a towel,
and step into the steam.

The hot water feels great
on my neck muscles.
I close my eyes
and drown my head.
My shoulders relax.

Suddenly, I get a sense
I'm not alone.
The soothing hot water
feels freezing cold.

I open my eyes.
Dude shapes
in the steam.

I expect to see
Jim and Pete,
but they're not there.

I keep my eyes up
above the neck.
I'm not homophobic;
I just don't want to see
or compare.

A body brushes against me.
I jerk away.

       "You sucked today."

"Yeah, Needlemier,
but the sun'll come out tomorrow."

       "What?"

"Nothing."

G'ma always said that . . .
actually she sang it,
but she's not here
and I'm not either.

I dart out of the shower
so fast, the steam
still holds my profile.

I get back to my locker
and towel off.

Crap!
My boxers are
on the ground,
all wet and manky.
I must've dropped them
when I went to shower.

I make sure no one's watching,
then stuff them into my backpack.
I'll have to go commando.

My jeans feel weird against
my nuts.
I hold my cock
to one side as I zip them up.

Don't want to get my foreskin
caught in the zipper.

Don't even want to think about that.

Musical Chairs

I'm almost late to Bio
because I spent too long
in front of the mirror
messing with my hair.

I halt just inside the door.
The seat's empty next to Bender.

I pull off my backpack
and head toward Ollie's table.

I've just about got my book out,
when I stumble.

Great.
The entire contents of my backpack
spill out onto the floor.

    "Way to go, Stout."

I'm sure everyone's laughing,
but I don't hear them or notice or care.

Shasten's sitting at the table next to Ollie.
In my seat.

I put my backpack on the floor
between them and pull an empty chair over.

    "You forget something?"

Shasten points behind me.
My books and shit are still on the floor.

Freeze-frame me.

Holy shit!
My boxers are on the floor!
Again!

I rush over and stuff them in my pocket.
Then I step on my tube of zit cream.
Looks like I just jizzed all over my shoe.

Oh, man.
What's she doing at my table?

Start my heart.

    "Here."
    Shasten hands me a tissue.

I wipe off all the white goo.

"So did Bender forget deodorant, or what?"

    "No. Well, maybe.
    I don't like getting that close."

We giggle. Ollie snorts.

    "They have three people already,
    and I want to get an A in this class."

"Oh, so you want to sit with the smart people."

    "Yes I do."
    Shasten winks at Ollie.

Ollie chitters like a chipmunk.

At the front of the room,
Mr. Lipston pulls down a white video screen.
He switches off the lights,
then starts a PowerPoint.

The projector flashes a picture of a brain,
then the screen goes black.

> "Did you see that, class?
> What was it?"

"A brain," we reply.

> "And where's the image of the brain now?"

> "In our heads," Ollie says.

> "In your pants more like,"
> Bender mutters.

Stifled laughs from the class.

Mr. Lipston doesn't seem to notice.

> "That image of the brain,
> that particular memory,
> is now in your
> frontal lobe."

The brain flashes on the screen again.

"Your brain's made up of different lobes.
The frontal lobe
is responsible for processing
and storing your memories."

"I guess I should remember that."

"It'll probably be on the test,"
Shasten says.

I suddenly feel
a soft hand on my arm
in the dark.

"Are you okay with me sitting here?"

"Oh, yeah, sure. Why?"

"Good. It's just that
you seem sort of distracted."

Freeze-frame me.

Distracted?
Understatement of the century.
I can't even begin to explain
how her touch feels.

The pads of her fingers,
the palm of her hand,
so soft, so warm.

But there's something else too.
A quality in her touch,
like I can almost *feel* her thoughts.

Uh-oh. Crotch movement.
I can't control it.
Got to stop the erection.

Penguins, penguins, penguins
on an iceberg.

I focus on the least sexy thing in my world.
Penguins on an iceberg.

I try to settle down,
but my heart's pounding.
Penguins . . .

There's something about Shasten.
Like she's radioactive.
Not in a lose-your-hair-
putrid-boils-erupt-on-your-skin
sort of radioactive.
More like the-smell-of-brownies-baking-
after-you've-drunk-mega-Red-Bull-
while-watching-Shaun-White-
compete-for-his-third-gold-medal-in-the-
Winter-Olympics-half-pipe-competition
sort of radioactive.

I can't stop vibrating.

The lights come back on.
I can't believe class is almost over.

I look down at my notebook.
There are only two words on the page.

Frontal lobe.

Lunchables

Creative Writing is getting stressful.
We have to read our homework
out loud in front of the class.

Mrs. Long likes how I wrote,
"His weathered skin is
like the bark of an ancient tree."

I'm not sure Jack Hoobie
would be as appreciative.

I rush out of class for lunch.
I'm hungry, but not for food.

I search the cafeteria,
then the main quad outside.
No Shasten.

Ollie's at the tree by himself.
I plop down next to him
and open my bag lunch.

> "Is this going to be a thing?"
> His big eyes are hopeful and fearful.

"A thing?"

> "Well, I sort of figured yesterday's lunch
> was a fluke."

"It wasn't a fluke."

> "Be honest, you weren't
> searching for me just now."

"Well, no.
But does that mean
I can't have lunch
with you today?"

     "No. But I need to know if
     this is going to be a thing,
     or will you be moving on
     when someone more popular
     shows up?"

"Is there anyone
more popular than you, Oll?"

Ollie does his chipmunk chitter,
then stops abruptly.

     "Dude.
     I need to know.
     Misunderstandings are best
     avoided when expectations are met."

Before I can reply,
Ollie's eyes glaze over.
I turn.
Shasten's sauntering toward us.

     "So is this a thing?"
     Shasten asks us.

I burst out with a laugh.

"Okay, okay.
This is a thing!"

I elbow Ollie.

Shasten sits down next to me.
She wraps her legs up in a bowtie.

"That looks painful."

> "What, the lotus position?
> Then, avert your eyes."

"You eating anything?"

> "Not that, whatever it is."
> Shasten sneers at my SPAM-wich.

> "So should we schedule a
> Bio study group, William?"

"That's a great idea, Oll, yeah."

> "After school might be a problem for me,"
> Shasten says.

The look in her eyes
warns me away from any attempts at witty.

> "I've got a job in the evenings
> that I really need to keep."

> "How about before school?"

I'm not much of an early riser,
but I'd do it if it meant some
quality time with Shasten.

Needlemier walks over.

"There's my cue. I'm outta here."
Ollie gathers up his stuff.

"What's all this?" Needlemier asks
as Ollie leaves.

"We're team Bio," Shasten says.

"Yeah, Bender told me."

I can see he's agitated.
He keeps his eyes on Shasten.
Like I'm not even here.

The bell rings, saving us
from an awkward silence.

Needlemier gestures to Shasten.
"Come."

Shasten cocks her head.
"I'm not your dog, Bradley."

"Yeah, yeah."

She walks away next to him,
but not exactly with him.
Needlemier tosses a weird look back at me.

I can't tell if it's anger
or something else.

Stats

We each get assigned
a computer in class.

This is cool.
School-supplied computers
with Internet connections.
J-Bob will not believe this.

Our teacher wants us
to find a pool
of data.

Something that's meaningful
to us.

The kid next to me is
looking up baseball stats.

The kid in front of me
is looking up video game sales.

I keep thinking of Patches
and what he said to me.

I search on "Missing Kids."

There are 84,924 open cases
of missing children
under the age of eighteen
in the FBI's National Crime Information Center.

I search on "Child Abuse."

There are more than three million
reports of child abuse
in the United States
every year.

More than 3.3 million reports
of child sexual exploitation to
the Cyber Tip Line.

Child sexual exploitation?

WTF?

The teacher walks toward me.

I search on "hockey,"
then clear my browser history.

Art History

Movie day!
I love movie days.

I wonder if teachers feel the same
way about movie days.

> Mr. Perry waves at me.
> "Would you be so kind
> as to close the curtains?"

"Sure."

This room must've been
some sort of workshop
before it was a classroom.
One wall is all glass windows above
waist-high counters.

The industrial curtains
are heavy and made
from some rubbery material.
They hang from
the ceiling in tracks
and almost touch the floor.

I pull them across
the wall of windows.

The room goes dark
just as the movie starts.

In the dark you don't actually
have to pay attention.

I stay at the windows,
holding the curtains.

An image of a skull
composed of naked women
flashes on the screen.

It catches me off guard.

The boobs and the butts
make me uncomfortable,
but it's a really cool
composition.

Surrealism. Salvador Dali.
His art's really odd,
but I like it.

A giggle outside the window.

I pull myself back around
the curtains.

A flash of red.
A little kid's hiding in the bushes
underneath the classroom windows
across the walkway.

"Patches," I whisper.

I wave at him,
but he's looking into the
window of the classroom
across from mine.

I look back into my dark
classroom.
I have to wait a sec
for my eyes to adjust.

Everyone's absorbed in the movie.
Mr. Perry's facing the screen,
but I can tell by the slight head bob
that he's totally napping.

I pull myself behind the curtain
and draw it around me
like a cape.

I slide my butt
up onto the counter.

The windows open
outward.

I back my legs out,
then let go, waiting
for the gravity to help
pull me down,
but my belt buckle catches
on the latch.

I fumble at the buckle.
It slips free,
and I drop
to the ground.

Ditchin'

I look up and
down the walkway.
No kids.
No adults.
No teachers.

I cross the grass
to the bushes
under the window
where Patches had been.

"Patches?"

What had he been looking at?
I peek inside the classroom,
drop down as the teacher
passes by the window.

Then I see red flashing
through the bushes.

I push forward through the brush
but lose sight of him again.

Then, rustling.

He's moving away from me.

"Patches, wait!"
I call as loud as I dare.

I follow the rustling.
Around the corner.

Where'd he go?

Quick footsteps behind me.

Patches darts down the walkway.
I must've passed him?

I take off after him.

He's very fast for a little dude,
and he's got a big head start.

I get to the parking lot.
Patches is darting
between parked cars.

I give chase.
Patches pauses
between SUVs,
but when I get there,
he's gone.

"Come on, kid!"

I drop to the pavement
and peer under the cars.

There are his sneakers
trotting toward the street.
I leap up and dash after him.

I have to pause at the crosswalk.
Cars are filling the street outside the school,
gearing up for the daily pickup.

I finally get across the street,
but now where?

Why's this kid out on his own
all the time?

Shouldn't he be
in day care or school?
There's his red shirt;
he's down the street
near a tall gnarled tree.

I run after him,
then stop by the tree.

He's vanished again,
but there's no place for him to hide.

"Where are you?
Are you okay?
That stuff you told me the other day—"

        "I am the hider.
        You are the troubled seeker.
        Your storm is coming."

There he is!
Up in the tree.

"Hey, show yourself.
I won't hurt you."

I walk around the base of the tree,
peering up through branches
that are knotted and bent
like a bodybuilder's arms.

How'd he get up there?

At the back of the tree,
I see strips of wood
nailed into the trunk:
a ladder for
small feet and tiny hands.

    "You forgot something."

I jerk around.
Shasten has my backpack
on her slim shoulders.

"Oh, uh . . . thanks."
I walk over to her
and take the backpack.
"How did you get this?"

    "I saw you climb out the window."

"You did?"

"I never figured you for a ditcher."

"I'm not.
I was going to go back
before the bell."

"School's been out for twenty minutes."

"What? No way."
I look at my phone
It's three-thirty.
I've been gone for over an hour?
It seems more like ten minutes.

"When I didn't see you come back,
I went and got your stuff."

"Thanks for bringing it."

"What were you looking for
in the bushes
outside my class?"

"I was looking for this little kid."
I point up the tree.

"What little kid?"

Just past the tree,
a bunch of little kids
are crossing the street.
I just catch a glimpse
of a red shirt
mixing in.

"There. That kid,
the one with the red shirt."

It's a preschool class.
Some hop, some skip,
some trudge.
Patches vanishes
inside the flock.

"I don't see him now."

        "Oh, no. I'm late!
        I've gotta go.
        Hope you find him."

Shasten rushes away.
She's all serpentine and glorious,
even when she's in a hurry.

Did Patches escape
from his preschool class?

I need to let them know.
They should keep
a better eye
on him.

Buckaroo Preschool

I trot after the group of kids.
They gather at a little park,
waiting for their parents to pick them up.

The shiny sedans and SUVs
roll up, pick up, and drive off
in a choreographed assembly line.

I search the constantly moving
group of kids.
No Patches.
WTF?

There's a woman wearing a neon pink cap
in the middle of the kids.
Must be the teacher.
No one else would wear that color.

"Hi, do you have a little boy
named Patches in your school?"

       "And who are you?"

"Oh, I'm William."
I stick my hand out,
but she doesn't return
my offer.

       "Well, William,
       do you have a family member
       attending our school?"

"Um, no."

She doesn't understand
why I'm asking.
How could she?

"I'm only asking
because I saw
this little boy
running around
all alone."

> "If he was alone,
> then I'm sure he doesn't
> attend Buckaroo Preschool."

"You sure?
Maybe he goes
by another name?"

> "Even if he did, I can't give out
> that sort of information."

"He joined your group
when you crossed the street
back there. He's wearing a
red flannel shirt."

> "Are you his brother?"

"No, just a friend."

"What did you say
your last name was,
William?"

"I didn't."

She's getting weird.
I need to go.

I turn and walk off.

Mustang Ask

I am still searching for Patches
when a car honks
and rolls up beside me.

It's Coach Harmon
in a clean old mustang.

      "Hey, Flash. Need a ride?"

"Sure, why not?"

I get in.
The leather's nice.
Black with white cross-stitching.
The engine thumps a low growl.

"V8?"

      "Five full liters."

"Sweet."

      "Where to?"

"Heil Ave would be great."

I'm digging riding in his car.
I wish someone would see me,
but I don't really know anyone to impress,
except maybe Shasten.

      "What've you been doing?"

"Looking for . . ."

If I tell him I'm searching
for a little boy,
he might get the wrong idea.

". . . a job.
One of my dad's
requirements."

> "Well, working builds character.
> But then, so does team sports."

"Yeah?"

> "Did you play anything in Kansas?"

"No.
Lived too far from school."

> "Well, now that you're here,
> would you consider playing football?"

"Football? Um, I don't know."

> "You're pretty fast.
> I think you could be good,
> with my help."

"They assign a lot of homework here."

> "Remember what I told you
> about reputation?"

"Yeah.
About getting a rep early."

"Well, it's true.
You can be a dweeb
or a popular."

"I'm not sure I want to be either."

"How 'bout just plain cool then?"

"That would work."

"Well, football will set you up.
If you were on the team
and played hard,
you'd be cool."

"Yeah, but don't the uniforms cost?"

"Don't worry 'bout that.
Let's see how you do first."

"I don't know . . ."

"Did I mention
you'd be popular with the girls?"

Freeze-frame me.

Girls?

Like the sun-drenched-
Dip-Cone girls?
Like Shasten?
She seems to like the meatheads,
Bender and Needlemier.

"When's practice?"

> "Every day
> after school
> until winter break."

If I did some homework at lunch,
and the rest before I went to bed,
I could probably manage.
But wait.
House Rule 4.

"I can't.
I have to get a job."

> "Saving for college?"

"It's my dad's condition
for me staying here."

> "I got ya.
> Let's say I can get you a job,
> will you at least come to the tryouts?"

"Yeah, I guess that would be okay."

We get to Heil Avenue.

"Hey, can you drop me here?"

He pulls over in front
of some fancy apartments.

"You live here?"

"No. But I have to do a thing."

"Okay. Tryouts are in two days."

"I'll be there,
if you can get me the job."

"Can do, Flash.
Trust me."

The Mustang rumbles away.

I don't know why,
but I don't want him to know
exactly where I live.

Maybe it's more
I don't want my dad to see
me drive up in a fast car
with some dude at the wheel.

No Worries

I guess I didn't
have to worry
about being seen.
There's no one home.

No pickup.
No note.
No dinner.
No nothing.

I drop my backpack
and pull out my books.

I settle onto my cot
and read a chapter
about the brain.

I put in my ear buds
and listen to some
dubstep radio.

Music helps me focus,
but sometimes it helps me
drift off to daydreams.

Homecoming Fantasy

I emerge from a long dark tunnel.
Black helmet.
Black jersey: 00
The name on the back: FLASH

I stomp onto the sideline.

The crowd gasps.
They whisper, "It's Flash,
it's Flash, it's Flash,"
as I walk past the stands.

We're down seven points now,
and our guys are desperate.
Bender's injured.
Time-out.

       "Get in there, Flash,"
       Coach says with relief.

I step onto the field,
low-five Bender as he hops off.

They snap the ball.

They have to pass.
I read it and blitz.
Their line's caught off guard.
I've got a clear path.

I bowl their quarterback over.

Fumble!

I gather up the ball and run,
outpacing their players.
The crowd cries,
"Go! Flash! Go!"

Touchdown!

Cheers from the crowd.
One cheer stands out from the rest.
It's Shasten.
She's yelling something in Swedish
that I can't understand.

We run to the sidelines
to let the kicking team on.

"Coach, let's go for the win!"

     "I don't know, Flash."

     "Let us try," says Needlemier.

Coach nods.

Needlemier and I
rush back onto the field.

The crowd roars.
They know what we're going to do,
but the other team doesn't.

Salcido sets up for the field goal,
Needlemier to hold.
I'm at the line
set out wide.

We snap the ball.

Salcido fakes the kick.
Needlemier drops back to pass,
but our line falters.

I reverse.
Needlemier's hit.
He laterals the ball.
I snatch it out of midair
and tuck it under my arm.
I turn on the jets.

I'm hit at the sideline,
but leap toward the goal.
I hold out the ball
just inside the marker.

The crowd hushes.

The ref puts the whistle to his lips
and signals.

Score!

We win
by one point.

The team lifts me into the air.
I look down
at the crowd.

Shasten's crying.
She's still yelling in Swedish.
I think it means, "I love you."

Ouch!

My toe kicks the sink.
I snap out of my fantasy.
Fucking sink!

I stare at the sink
for the length of a song.
I come up with a solution.
I'll just need some duct tape.

No-Fly Zone

I search the drawers
in the kitchen.
I find masking tape,
blue painter's tape,
and black electrical tape.

They might work, but
not so well.

I finally find a ratty
roll of duct tape.
But it's weird—
it's got a pastel floral design
with pink and blue and green.
It doesn't seem to fit
in my father's man cave.

I poke around to find
a towel or a sponge,
but the sponges are worn
and the towels are too thin.

I wonder what's upstairs.
I know I'm not supposed
to go up there,
but how would he know
if I did?

I go up the stairs slowly,
looking for laser beams
or wi-fi surveillance cameras.

But now I know he works
for the TSA and not the NSA.
So I'm not surprised to find
only a creak
in the third step
from the top
as a form of lame security.

Unlike the rest of the house,
the upstairs is extraordinarily neat.

At the top of the stairs
to the right,
there's a bathroom
that looks like
it's never been used.

Blue-and-light-brown tile
of some sort that
I'm pretty sure is expensive.
Some of the tiles have
designs in them.
Yellow sunflowers,
a green turtle,
a brown owl—
nothing that seems to fit his taste.

I creep down the hallway.
The first bedroom must be his;
it reeks of bourbon and cigarettes.

It's small and only sort of messy.
The bed isn't made.
There's a deep butt-shaped
dent in the mattress.

A half-empty bottle of Maker's Mark
rests on the nightstand
next to an ashtray
overflowing with butts.

The walls have
sun-bleached
rectangle-shaped outlines
from missing picture frames.

I back out
and close the door.
Feels wrong
to be in his space.

I open a cupboard
in the hallway.
and find what I've
been searching for.

Towels.
I pull a hand towel
from the bottom of a pile.
He won't miss it.

I'm about to
head downstairs
when I see another door
at the end of the hallway.

My heart says, "Leave,"
but my curiosity begs to be satisfied.
My brain rationalizes . . .
You're already here.
What's the harm
in taking a peek?

I pause at the door.
There's a small ornate sign
hanging on it about chest high
that reads CAMELOT.

I put my hand on the knob.

Then I hear the front door opening downstairs.

Shit!
I spin around
and bolt to the stairs.
Too late.
He's coming up.

I duck into the bathroom
just as that third step creaks.

I squeeze myself behind the open door.

He pauses outside
the bathroom.
I hold my breath.

His bedroom door opens,
then closes.

I let out my breath.
Wait.

Does he know I'm up here?
Did he open and close
his door just to catch me?
Is he waiting for me
in the hallway?

I can't move.

A *thump* comes from his room.
I peek out.
The hallway's empty.

I dart down the stairs,
making sure
I miss the
third step.

My feet hit
the ground floor,
I open the front door,
then spin around,
slamming it behind me.

      "What the hell are you doing?"

"Oh, hi."

He's at the top of the stairs,
glaring down,
shoes off,
shirt unbuttoned.

"Just back from a jog."
I'm sweating like
Niagara Falls and
hope that helps sell it.

His eyes drop to my hand.
I forgot I have the towel.

I wipe my sweaty forehead.

> "Try to keep the noise down,
> will ya?"

He turns around.

"Yes, sir."

Phew, I think he bought it.

Sink Fix

I lie on my cot
with my head
under the sink.

Why am I
not allowed upstairs?

I roll up the towel.

Is he an alcoholic?

I wrap a strip
of duct tape
around each end
of the towel.

Why is that bathroom
never used?

The last bits
of duct tape
hold the rolled towel
in place
under the edge of the sink.

What happened to
the pictures on the wall?

I lift my head
and bump the towel.
Feels like a pillow.

What in the hell is Camelot?

Camelot
was the name of King Arthur's
castle and court.
I think King Arthur was killed.

I read in my American History book
that "Camelot" was used to describe
John F. Kennedy's presidency.
That didn't end well for him either.

I spin around
and put my feet up
on the cot.

Big toe on towel.
Yay. I beat the sink problem.

What's behind that door?

Dinner of No Returns

Grocery store
roasted chicken
and canned corn.

Not that bad actually,
but nowhere as good
as G'ma's worst
meatloaf.

I can't complain.
It's a free meal.

I smell bourbon
coming out
of his skin,
or maybe it's
coming from his
ever-present
commuter cup.

He points
and grunts
his side of the
dinner conversation.

I reply with smiles
and nods
while I pass him
the corn
or the chicken.

I can't stop wondering
what might be
up in that room.

What's he hiding?

Is it the same thing
he's drowning
with bourbon?

　　"I gotta go."

"Okay. I'll do the dishes."

He nods,
grunts his approval,
then walks out.

I listen for the front door to close,
but instead the TV comes on.

"Aren't you going to work?"

　　　"No, it's game night."

He lights up a cigarette
and flips through the channels
with the remote.

The TV screen
fills with channel listings.
He finally settles on
Cowboys versus Steelers.

　　　"Hey, the dishes?"

"Right."

We only used two plates and two forks.
Cleanup's quick.

I guess he doesn't want me
to watch the game with him.
That's fine with me.
It's getting late,
and I still have
homework to do.

A Wicked Gothic Thing

It's foggy out.
Thick-like-whipped-cream
foggy.

I'm pretty sure
my school's on
this street.
Pretty sure.

I've been walking
for twenty minutes,
but there's no
line of mommy cars
and no Mini Mart.
on the corner.

There's a weird
high-pitched sound.
A grinding, like metal
against metal.

I push forward.
A merry-go-round
emerges out of the fog.

It's not a cheerful
carnival sort of
merry-go-round.

It's a wicked gothic thing.
Instead of horses
and swans
to ride,
there are dragons
and minotaurs
with black
iron saddles.

No calliope
oompah-oompah.
Just the sound
of metal grinding
on metal
as the monsters
spin.

I walk up closer.
The dragons
are breathing
tongues of flame.
The minotaurs
are blowing
puffs of steam.

As the gothic
parade spins past,
they all glare
down at me
and gnash their
pointed teeth.

A golden dragon
catches my attention.

I step up onto the
spinning platform.

The golden dragon
bows her head
as I approach.

She unfolds her wings,
reveals
a gold saddle
on her back.

I climb up
and settle in.

We're spinning
much faster than before.

The minotaurs are
grunting.
The dragons are
hissing.

Faster we spin.
The world beyond
the merry-go-round
is a blur.

Something big
grabs me from behind.

A huge black minotaur
pulls me off the golden dragon
and pins me to the platform.

I can't get away.
His arms are so strong.

He holds me tight.
His rough beard
scratches my cheek.

His strong hands
claw at my pants.

My pants are dragged down.
The minotaur's nails
dig into my butt cheeks.

I kick something soft
yet solid.

I wake screaming.

Screams

My Bio book falls
off my chest.
I switch off my
reading light.

It was a dream.
Just a dream.

Then I hear
a faint shrill scream.

It's not me.

It's thin and distant,
coming from inside the wall.

I strain to hear
the screaming.

It stops,
then starts suddenly,
then stops,
then starts again.

Did someone leave
the tea kettle
on the stove?

I go into the kitchen.

No tea kettle.

The fitful screaming's
coming from the vent
above the stove,
and it's louder now.

Is it the wind?
Is it a kitten?

No. I know what it is.
It's a kid.

It's coming from inside the house.
It's coming from upstairs.

I get to the top of the stairs.

But then the screaming stops.

The night's so still,
I can hear my own
heart beating.

> "Daddy, stop it.
> It hurts."

What the hell?
I move down the hall.
Past the bathroom.
Past his bedroom.
Without thinking.

I place my hand on the knob
and open the door
to Camelot.

Camelot

A mural of a white stone castle
with moats and bridges and horses
covers the entire wall.
The ceiling's painted
with stars, fluffy clouds, and a full moon
in a dark-blue night sky.

A small bed
with a sheer white canopy
sits in the middle of the room,
a matching dresser against one wall.

Miniature plastic horses
of different colors
and sizes
line the shelves
and dresser top.

There are prancing horses,
grazing horses,
dancing horses,
and even some unicorns
in the collection.

This is totally a little
girl's room,
a little girl's room that's never
been lived in.

I'm suddenly blinded
by a bright white light.

I hear the scream
between my ears
followed by
a whispered,
"Daddy, it hurts."

The light
pulls away
from my eyes
and takes the shape of
a silver orb.

The orb floats
and dances
like a firefly
landing in the middle
of the white bed.

Silence.

A total vacuum of sound
as if I'm in outer space.

I must still be dreaming.
Of course I am . . .

  "What the hell are you doing in here?"

Shit!

"What.
Are.
You.
Doing.
In.
Here?"

The bourbon's oozing
out his pores.
He steps into the moonlight.
His face contorts.
His intensity rises
from anger to rage.

"I'm sorry, I just . . .
I heard a scream.
A girl."

His face melts.
He staggers
toward me
as if he's been hit
in the gut.

"What? What did you say?"

"A girl.
She said,
'Daddy, stop it.
It hurts.'"

My words
make him shake.
He leans against the wall,
then crumples to a sitting position.

"What happened here?"

He doesn't respond.
His eyes twitch.
He's visualizing
something from his past.

"What happened?"

His eyes jerk up.

> "This is my . . .
> my daughter's room."

Castles and Horses

I'm suddenly a little
unsteady myself.
I plop down
on the floor
in front of him.

I've got a sister?
How old is she?
Where is she?
What's going on?

Before I can
voice my million questions,
he begins
to talk.

> "About thirteen years ago,
> a few months after your mom and I split,
> I met a woman.
> Sarah was my sponsor."

"Sponsor?"

> "Yeah, from rehab.
> She saved me more than once
> from falling off the wagon."

So he tried to stop the drinking before.

> "We got married after I was sober a year.
> Jessica was born on our first anniversary.
> Jess loved castles and horses
> as you can see."

He picks up
two horses
off the shelf.
I'm shocked when
he makes them
trot around
in the air in front of him,
just like a kid playing.

"Jess would laugh and laugh
when I did this.
She loved to watch them prance."

He continues to play with the horses,
making them buck and prance.

"She was my sunshine,
my joy."

"What hurt her?
Why was she screaming?"

"I couldn't stop it.
She pleaded with me,
but I couldn't stop it."

Uh-oh. Is he
some sort of pervert?
A goddamned sicko pedophile?

"What did you . . .
what did you *do* to her?"

"No! No! It's not what I did to her.
It's what I couldn't do *for* her.
I couldn't take away her pain."

He's got the two horses
prancing in front of his face.

"But Sarah could.
Sarah took away Jess's pain.
Forever."

"How?"

"You should know the why
before you can understand the how."

"Okay, so tell me why."

"Jess had a severe case of Brittle Bone Disease.
It had gotten so bad that
by her eighth birthday,
if she walked, her legs would break,
if she played with her horses,
her arms would break.
Her pain was absolutely unbearable."

He continues to make
the plastic horses
dance around
in midair.

"We couldn't stand to see Jess
in so much pain and it was getting worse.
One night, Sarah gave Jess something
to help her sleep, but Jess never woke up.
She died . . . of an overdose. My angel . . ."

"Holy shit!"

"She killed her.
Sarah killed my little girl.
Her own little girl."

"I'm so sorry."

"Me too, yet sorry is never enough."

"What happened to Sarah?"

My dad's sad eyes
lock with mine.

"Guilt's like a cup of really hot coffee.
It's impossible to hold tightly.
And even though it's light,
over time it becomes so heavy
that you'd do anything
to rid yourself of the weight.
Sarah found a way.
Sarah always found a way."

I'm afraid to ask,
but I have to.
"How?"

"She killed herself."

Jesus.

He crushes
the two plastic horses
in his fist.

Dad begins to sob.

I feel like a total jerk.
No wonder he never
came to visit.
No wonder he couldn't take me.
I can't hate this man.

Yup, tonight,
beginning right now,
he's my dad.

I wrap my arms around Dad
and hug him
with all I've got.

Mourning Counseling Session

I sit in the
uncomfortable
wooden chair
next to the water pitcher
and the box of tissues.

I watch Jill Archer
tidy up her desk.

I don't know
what to make
of last night's revelations.

I no longer
hate the man
I now call Dad.

But for some strange reason,
I don't yet love him.
Not quite yet.

When I was twelve,
I won a ribbon
for my sketch of a soldier.
I asked why my dad wasn't there
to see me win.
Gramps told me,
"Your dad's been dealt a bad hand."

I didn't understand
what he meant then,
but I do now.

Dad couldn't handle
another kid in his house,
not with all that shit going on.

I'm not sure
he can
even now.

       "William? Are you
       getting enough sleep?"

"Yeah, I guess, why?"

       "Your eyes are so bloodshot."

"Hay fever."

I can't let her know
that I spent all night
hugging my father
to sleep
in the bedroom
of his daughter
who was mercy
killed by his
suicidal wife.

Nope. Not going there.

       "So how are you getting along?
       Made any new friends?"

"I have actually."

She jots down notes.

"Ollie Goligowski for one."

> "Olliver? The gamer kid
> with the glasses?"

"Yup. Him."

> "Really? Why Olliver?"

"He's smart.
And he's funny
in an odd way."

> "I'm surprised.
> I figured you for,
> I don't know,
> someone more . . ."

"Normal?"

> "No. Someone more
> like yourself."

"Like me?"

> "Athletic, attractive."

She finds me attractive?
We must've asked
ourselves the same question
at the same time.

She blushes bright pink.

> "Strike that.
> Let's get back to
> why you like Olliver."

"Ollie's insightful.
He understands his
shortcomings,
but he doesn't whine about them.
I like that about him."

> "Have you made any enemies?"

"God,
I hope not."

> "Let me rephrase that."

She sounds like a
TV attorney
cross-examining
a hostile witness.

> "Have you had any run-ins
> with anyone?"

"Run-ins?"

> "Fights."

"I know what it means."

Why's she asking me this?

I battle with Needlemier,
but I wouldn't call them fights.
Has he complained?
What a whimp-ass.

"Some chest thumping,
but fights? Nope.
Why are you asking?"

       "A middle school boy got his
       collarbone broken last week."

Freeze-frame me.

She's gotta be talking about
Red.
Does she know him?
Does she know I'm the one?
Is she giving me a chance
to come clean?
Should I?
I can say I didn't know I injured him.

What am I thinking?
Red and those asswipes
were in the wrong.
They were beating up a kid.
He pulled a knife on me.

The truth is
they attacked Andy,
then me.

I was *protecting* Andy.

Andy'll back me.

Wait, Andy's mom
must think I did it.
Andy never saw me
return his stuff.

What should I do?

"The boy hasn't
described the attacker,
only said that he was older."

Good.
Maybe it's not
even Red
she's talking about.
I shrug
and keep
my eyes
locked
with hers.

"You do recall
that anything you tell
me stays in this room, right?
You're safe here."

Yes,
I'm safe.
Especially if
I keep
my
mouth
shut.

Weight Room

No flag football today,
so I won't get a chance
to avenge our loss the other day.

Instead, we get to weightlift.
I've never done much before.
My old school didn't have
a good gym,
or anything else.

Bender and Needlemier
are showing off
of course.
They load up
the weights
on the bench press.

Bender grunts
and groans
like a grizzly bear.
Needlemier
spots for him.

> "That's one-seventy-five, man!
> Come on. One more."

Like everyone
needs to know
how much they
can lift.

I head to the
weights.

Jim's there with Pete.

"Careful, it's at
two hundred pounds."

"That's okay, Jimbo!"
I stoop under the bar,
then lift it onto
my shoulders

I squat down,
press up,
and stop.

"Y'all are fucking
with me."

"Why, what's wrong?"

"Come on, Pete.
It's too light."

Jim slips on
two plates.

"Try that."

I lift it,
squat,
then press again.

"Come on, guys.
It's like a feather."

"We put on fifty more pounds, dude."

"More."

Pete slides
on a couple
of fifteen-pound plates.

I lift ten reps
and stop.

"More."

Coach walks over.

"What's going on?"

"William's already at
three hundred and fifty pounds."

"I can do more."

"Okay, Flash, but if you feel
something strain, stop."

"Coach, we're out of weights."

"Take some from those two."

Jim and Pete take some weights
from Bender and Needlemier.

The entire class is watching me now.

"What's he at?"
Needlemier asks.

"Four-twenty."

I press twenty reps.
The last one's hard,
but I get it up.

"You okay, Flash?"

"Nothing to it, Coach."

I'm not trying
to show off.
I just know
I can do more.

I press another ten.

"Wow," Pete says.

I get to twenty
more reps
and I know I'm done.

"Impressive, Flash."

"Strong thighs, so what?"
Bender says.

"When he sets his feet
and drives through the line,
you'll not want to be in his way.
That's what," Coach replies.

Biology of Shasten

I get to Bio
on time,
but not
before
Ollie or Shasten.

They're both
already at our table.

Ollie's working
on his iPad,
or so he'd like her to believe.
Every few seconds
Ollie takes a selfie
with Shasten unaware.

He's really enjoying
sitting next to her.

His smile makes him
look like the Cheshire Cat.

His plump shape,
big eyes, and glasses
make him look more like
the Cheshire Turtle.

Shasten's reading the textbook.
She looks tired.

"Hi."

          "Hang on. Last page."

Weird.
I don't know
how I know,
but I know
she's tense.

"Just trying to finish the chapter
before class starts."

"Shouldn't you
have done that
last night?"

"Yeah, but I had to work late."

It's as if I can
hear her
muscles
tighten ever
so slightly.

She's not annoyed.
She's not upset.
But she's agitated.

She highlights
something
in the book,
then closes it.

"You okay?
I get a sense
that you're stressed."

Shasten pauses.

She studies me with
her green-blue eyes.

"Exactly how do you *sense*
my stress?"

"I dunno.
I just do."

"Are you taking the piss?"

"What?
No.
Are my pants wet?"

"She means,
are you making fun of her?"
Ollie interjects.
"My grandmother's British.
She talks like that."

He shrugs
and goes back to
his iPad.

"Someone's told you about me, then."

"Huh?
Told me what?"

"That I *sense* things.
That I'm an empath."

Empathy

Gramps used to say,
"If you give someone
enough time,
even a sane person
will show you their crazy."

I've only known
Shasten for a week,
so does this mean
she is way crazy?

The only empath
I've ever heard of
was that
alien woman from
Star Trek: The Next Generation,
Deanna Troi.

And if I remember
correctly,
she'd get
headaches a lot.

Maybe Shasten's
an alien.
A serpentine alien.
Sweet.

We're supposed to be starting
lab work with microscopes.
Ollie's all business
and is totally ignoring us.

"So what exactly is
an empath?"

   "A highly sensitive person
   who feels the emotions of others."

"Cool.
Can you read my mind?"

   "No, not really."

"Good.
I'd be really
embarrassed
if you could."

   "Hey, can one of you switch
   on the illuminator?"

"Sure, Ollie."
I flip the switch,
and a little light brightens
under the microscope lens.

"So can you tell if I'm angry or sad?"

   "No, I don't think I can."

"Can you tell if I'm happy or excited?"

   "No, I don't think I can."

"Then how are you an empath again?"

   "Let me give you an example."

"See," says Ollie, "first you turn
the coarse focus knob,
and then you turn
the fine focus knob."

Ollie's a pig in shit with this Bio stuff.

"Take Olliver, for instance,"
Shasten says. "He's growing
frustrated."

"Yeah.
Well, that's kind of obvious."

Shasten folds
her arms
across her chest,
then focuses her eyes
at the next table.

"That blond girl
thinks you're cute.
The boy next to her
also thinks you're cute."

Shasten jerks her
face toward
the front
of the room.

"Mr. Lipston's enjoying
Kathy's low-cut top.

And the reason
why Kathy's wearing
that low-cut top
is because she's angry
at her father."

"If you can deduce all that,
then why can't you
tell if I'm happy
or sad?"

"I can *sense* all that.
And I don't know
why I can't sense you.
It's never happened before
that I can't sense someone.
But I do have a theory."

"Okay, so let's just say
you're an empath—"

"I *am* an empath."

"Where's my proof?
I mean, I could make up
things about people too."

"I don't just *make things up*."

"Can you guys stop arguing?"

"Should I believe her, Ollie?"

"Yes."

"Why?"

"Because I *am*
growing frustrated."

"Of course you are.
You're doing all the work."

"That's not why I'm frustrated though."

"No? Then why?"

"Because everyone knows
Shasten's an empath."

Well, I didn't.
Gramps was very Christian.
G'ma went along,
although she didn't
believe absolutely like Gramps did.
But then she never
faced death alone in a jungle.

"So what's your theory?
Why can you read
everyone else but not me?"

"Well, I believe
You're either working really hard
to block out something,
or you're an empath too."

"Right,
and may the farce be with you."

We finish our overview
of the microscope,
then identify
cell membranes,
nucleus, and
mitochondria
of pig muscle.

Somehow "the Golgi apparatus"
we're scrutinizing
under the microscope
becomes
"the Goligowski apparatus,"
which Ollie thinks is hysterical.

The bell rings and starts
the dash for the door.

I bump into Kathy
as we exit the room.

      "Nice top," Shasten says.

Kathy spins around.

      "Right?" she squeals. "My dad about
      birthed a hippo saying
      I had to return it.
      I keep it in my locker.
      He'll never know."

Shasten gives me a look.

"Doesn't prove a thing."

Twenty Questions

"So I have to ask, Shasten.
Are you dating Needlemier?"

      "That's a good question."

"That's not really an answer."

      "Well, we go out.
      We do things.
      But we don't . . . you know."

"You don't what?"

      "Make out or anything."

"I like that answer."

      "Now, I have a question for you.
      Have you ever had
      any empathic experiences?"

"I don't know.
What is that—
an *empathic experience*?"

      "Where you sense other people's emotions.
      Where you feel like you can tell what
      someone's going to say or do
      before they say or do it."

"I can't say I have.
Although,
how do you define *sense*?"

"For me, it differs from person to person.
Sometimes I see things
in flash forward. It's like skipping
ahead in a movie.
Sometimes I hear things."

Freeze-frame me.

I've heard a dead girl scream.
I've heard a dead girl speak.
Is that what Shasten's talking about?

I don't want to mention it, though.
Not right now.
I don't want to divulge
Dad's sad history.

Start my heart.

"That flash forward thing
could be very handy."

    "Yes, it can be."

"My turn now.
Are you ever going to
have lunch with me?"

    "Wish I could, but
    I have to go home for lunch."

"Do you have a dog to walk or something?"

    "I wish that were it."

"You're not much on details."

"Sorry. I forget you're new here."

"Well, I was beginning to think
you didn't like me."

"No. I do. I do."

The blush on her cheeks gives me hope.

"I mean.
It's not you.
My mom is really sick."

"Oh. I didn't know.
I'm sorry."

"I go home at lunch to check on her
and to help with my little brother."

"I shouldn't be so nosey."

"It's okay.
It's common knowledge."

She puts her hand on my wrist.

"The thing is, I do like you.
I just don't have time for you."

Distraction

I do my lunch thing
with Ollie
under the tree.

       "So what's your favorite game?"

"I don't know, Monopoly?
Kings in the Corner?"

       "What's Kings in the Corner?"

"Like Solitaire, but with a bunch of players."

       "What console's it for?"

"Console?
There's no console."

       "So it runs on your desktop?"

"It doesn't run on anything.
It's a card game, Ollie."

       "You play *card games*?
       Did you just wake up from a coma?"

"Wait, ask me the question again."

       "What are your favorite games?
       Like Halo or W.O.W.,
       PS or Xbox?"

"Oh, then, Angry Birds."

       "Argh. Forget I even asked."

Ollie's right.
Back in Kansas, we were frozen in
Gramps' time.
Living with Gramps and G'ma
was like being in a pop culture coma.

Ollie and I don't talk for a while.

The bell rings.
Shasten's late returning from lunch.
I hope things are okay with her mom.

History and Stats
go by in a blur.
I can't keep my focus
in Art History.

My eyes keep drifting
out the window
searching for any sign of
red flannel.

But no Patches.

Class is over.
School's out.

I've got a bunch of homework,
but I figure
I'll go look for a job.
I've got something I need to do first.

I walk over to
Buckaroo Preschool.

Kids are playing and laughing inside.

I linger
under the
gnarled tree.
I search
the branches.
No red flannel
No little boy voice.

The wooden
strips nailed
into the trunk
like ladder rungs
have names
scratched in them.

Bobbi Newland,
Cheri Tager,
Renee Bown,
but no Patches.

Buckaroo Preschool lets out.
A herd of littles emerges from
the open door.

They bunch up
behind some teachers,
waiting impatiently.

If I could just find Patches,
maybe I could get
him to talk to an adult.
Get him to talk about his abuse.

I don't see him . . .
Wait!
I catch a glimpse of red.
I hear a familiar giggle.

But then I see
the pink baseball cap.
It's that suspicious teacher.

I duck behind the tree
so she doesn't see me.

The herd passes by
under a cloud of
audible turbulence.

> "You will not find me.
> I am the one you buried.
> No saving me now."

It's definitely Patches.
But I don't want that teacher
to see me.

I follow the
Buckaroo Preschool
class across the street to the park.

Keeping a safe distance
so as not to
stir up any concerns.

One by one, their parents
pick them up.
Surely, I'll find Patches now.

"You again?"

Uh-oh.

Pink-Cap teacher.

I wave and smile,
hoping she won't
ask any more
questions.

"Do you live around here?"

Freeze-frame me.

If I don't answer,
it'll look like
I'm hiding something.
Plus, it's just plain rude.

But if I tell the truth,
she'll probably
think I'm a sicko pedophile
or some sort of crazed serial killer.

"Cat got your tongue?"

Start my heart.

She's obviously
been talking to
little kids
all day long.

"I'm just waiting for my ride."

I hope that satisfies her.
Once all the kids are gone,
she'll waddle
back to the preschool
and forget all about me.

That is, unless I can find Patches
and prove to her
I'm only trying to help.

I linger,
looking over
the thinning crowd
of kids.

But then Pink Cap
starts digging through
her purse,
glancing at me
the whole time.

She pulls out a phone,
then fumbles with the screen.
After a few failed attempts,
she points the camera end
toward me.

Shit!
I'm about to run
when a car honks.

Pink Cap and I both turn,
as a black Mustang
pulls up.

"Flash! Just who I was looking for."

"Hi! Glad you're here."

"Get in."

I get in just as Pink Cap
attempts to snap a pic.

Sheets

"You said if I found you a job,
you'd try out for football, right?"

"Yeah, but . . ."

"Tryouts are tomorrow.
So I found you a job."

What?
We pull into the parking lot
in front of a warehouse.
A sign above the entry reads
WHOLE-IS-TECH WELLNESS.

"What is this place?"

"Where you're gonna work."

We go inside.
It smells sickly sweet,
like incense
and flowers.

We get to the front desk,
on which there are several
glass plates holding
smoldering
gray leaves.

"Zillah, here's the kid
I told you about."

The woman behind
the desk has long
gray braids.

She studies me
as if she's
checking my
ripeness.

   "I see what you mean, Coach."

Coach pats my back.

    "I'm Zillah.
    Come with me."

    "Go on, Flash."

I shrug at Coach and
follow Zillah
down a long hallway.

We pass a bunch of
older people
wearing robes.

Off to one side,
in a large hall,
a very skinny woman's
leading people through
yoga poses.

We pass a couple of smaller rooms
with colorful massage tables,
lower tables with Buddha statues,
and smoldering incense.

"There's a lot of cleaning
that needs to be done every day."

Cleaning?
Like a janitor?
That doesn't
sound like fun.
In fact, that sounds
like work.

"Plus there's all the laundry."

Laundry?
Seriously?
I sleep between
a washer and dryer.
Is this some sort of theme?

We enter a small room
with an industrial-sized
washer and dryer.

I'd get no sleep here at all.

There are brooms,
mops, towels,
and unmarked
bottles of green stuff
next to a sink.

"We only use organic
cleaning agents here.
No bleach or chemicals."

"That sounds . . . healthy."

"We have four massage rooms,
a yoga studio,
a solarium upstairs."

"Solarium?"

"You'll see."

Freeze-frame me.

I'd been counting
on that job
at the surf shop.
If I worked there,
I could learn
to surf.

And I could
probably
get great deals
for my friends.

How cool would
I be then?

Plus, there
are those
sun-drenched
surf girls.

Here there only seems to
be pale old people
and it smells funny.

"Well . . . I dunno."

   "You don't seem excited.
   Coach said you needed a job, no?"

"Yeah, but . . .
it's not exactly my dream job."

   "But it is a job."

A door opens
down the hall
just ahead of me.

A short man emerges,
wearing a white robe
and a big smile.

   "Thank you, Mr. Zimmerman."

That voice!
I walk past the doorway,
peek in.

A girl's pulling the sheet off
a massage table.

It's Shasten.

"When can I start?"

Job Perks

I fill up the washer with
sheets, pillowcases,
and towels. Pour in one cup
of clear organic stuff and hit
Start.

Next, the massage rooms.
Grab up used towels, sheets,
and robes.

I hope to run into Shasten,
but she seems to have vanished.

Every trash can I pass,
I empty into the main bin.

When the first load's done,
I move the contents
into the dryer.

The second load's
all robes.

Zillah doesn't "believe
in vacuum cleaners,"
so I have to
sweep the floors with
a natural hemp broom.

I wipe everything down
and spray the sinks
with the green gunk.

Time to fold
the laundry.

Solarium

Last thing of the night—
the solarium.

Zillah says the solarium's
a place of quiet reflection.

I open the door and see why.

The entire roof's open.
The salty breeze tickles my skin.
The night sky's flecked with tiny stars.

Potted trees edge the space.
A water fountain trickles at one end.
A circular fire pit stands in the center
filled with sticks of incense.
There are comfy-looking sofas
and lounge chairs everywhere.

"Beautiful."
It comes out a whisper.

I don't even notice that I'm not alone.

"William?" Shasten says.
"Hey. What are you doing here?"

"Hey. I work here."

"What? Since when?"

"Since today."

"I work here too."

"Cool.
Coach Harmon got me this job,
so don't think I'm stalking you
or anything, okay?"

            "The thought never entered my mind.
            Well, okay maybe for just a second or two."

I hear the smile in her words.
My pulse leaps.

"So what exactly is your job here?"

            "Actually, I'm in training.
            I have two hundred more hours
            apprenticing as a body worker."

"A what?"

            "Sort of like a masseuse,
            but it's more of a spiritual thing."

"Like 'Come to Jesus'?"

            "Nope. More like moving energy."

"Moving energy?"

            "I can't really explain it,
            but I can show you."

She guides me
to one of the lounge chairs.

            "Take off your shirt."